LOST WORLDS, UNKNOWN HORIZONS

Books by ROBERT SILVERBERG

The Masks of Time
The Time Hoppers
Hawksbill Station
To Live Again
Recalled to Life
Starman's Quest
Tower of Glass
Earthmen and Strangers (*editor*)
Voyagers in Time (*editor*)
Men and Machines (*editor*)
Tomorrow's Worlds (*editor*)
Revolt on Alpha C
Lost Race of Mars
Time of the Great Freeze
Conquerors from the Darkness
Planet of Death
The Gate of Worlds
The Calibrated Alligator
Needle in a Timestack
To Open the Sky
Thorns
Worlds of Maybe: Seven Stories of Science Fiction (*editor*)
Mind to Mind (*editor*)
The Science Fiction Bestiary: Nine Stories of Science Fiction (*editor*)
The Day the Sun Stood Still (*compiler*)
Beyond Control (*editor*)
Chains of the Sea (*compiler*)
Deep Space: Eight Stories of Science Fiction (*editor*)
Sundance and Other Science Fiction Stories
Mutants: Eleven Stories of Science Fiction (*editor*)
Threads of Time: Three Original Novellas of Science Fiction (*compiler*)
Sunrise on Mercury and Other Science Fiction Stories
Explorers of Space: Eight Stories of Science Fiction (*editor*)
Strange Gifts: Eight Stories of Science Fiction (*editor*)
The Aliens: Seven Stories of Science Fiction (*editor*)
The Crystal Ship: Three Original Novellas of Science Fiction (*editor*)
The Shores of Tomorrow: Eight Stories of Science Fiction
Earth Is the Strangest Planet: Ten Stories of Science Fiction (*editor*)
Trips in Time: Nine Stories of Science Fiction (*editor*)

LOST WORLDS, UNKNOWN HORIZONS

NINE STORIES OF SCIENCE FICTION

edited by

ROBERT SILVERBERG

THOMAS NELSON INC., PUBLISHERS
Nashville   New York

No character in this book is intended to represent any actual person; all the incidents of the stories are entirely fictional in nature.

Copyright © 1978 by Robert Silverberg

All rights reserved under International and Pan-American Conventions. Published in Nashville, Tennessee, by Thomas Nelson Inc., Publishers, and simultaneously in Don Mills, Ontario, by Thomas Nelson & Sons (Canada) Limited. Manufactured in the United States of America.

First edition

Library of Congress Cataloging in Publication Data

Main entry under title:

Lost worlds, unknown horizons.

CONTENTS: Wells, H. G. The country of the blind.—Finney, J. The third level.—Smith, C. A. The city of the singing flame. [etc.]
  1. Science fiction, American.   2. Science fiction, English.
I. Silverberg, Robert.
PZ1.L86   [PS648.S3]   813'.0876   78–18345
ISBN 0–8407–6601–7

Acknowledgments

"The Third Level," by Jack Finney. Copyright 1950 by Jack Finney. Reprinted by permission of Harold Matson Co., Inc.

"The City of the Singing Flame," by Clark Ashton Smith. Copyright 1931 by Gernsback Publishers, Inc. Reprinted by permission of the author's estate and its agents, Scott Meredith Literary Agency, Inc.

"The Sunken Land," by Fritz Leiber. Copyright 1942, 1970, by Fritz Leiber. Reprinted by permission of the author and his agent, Robert P. Mills, Ltd.

"The Doom That Came to Sarnath," by H. P. Lovecraft. Copyright 1938 by Popular Fiction Publishing Co. Reprinted by permission of the author's estate and its agents, Scott Meredith Literary Agency, Inc.

"Trips," by Robert Silverberg. Copyright © 1974 by Robert Silverberg. Reprinted by permission of the author and his agents, Scott Meredith Literary Agency, Inc.

Contents

The Country of the Blind	H. G. Wells	11
The Third Level	Jack Finney	39
The City of the Singing Flame	Clark Ashton Smith	45
The Sunken Land	Fritz Leiber	67
The Balloon Tree	Edward Page Mitchell	87
The Doom That Came to Sarnath	H. P. Lovecraft	97
A Tale of the Ragged Mountains	Edgar Allan Poe	105
Phantas	Oliver Onions	117
Trips	Robert Silverberg	135

Introduction

Once upon a time the world was very large, and most of it was wholly unknown except to the people who happened to live in the undiscovered places, and maps were full of fantastic guesses about faraway lands, and there were rumors of countries inhabited by dragons and gryphons and men whose heads grew beneath their shoulders. And then everything was discovered—or practically everything—and it was left to the science-fiction writers to supply the fantasies of remote times and spaces that once were provided by geographers and historians.

And so came about this collection of strange and fantastic tales.

Science fiction is a literature of ideas, of social criticism, of technological ingenuity, and of a lot of other things, but mainly, I believe, it is a literature of wonder. Science-fiction writers work in the same tradition as Homer, whose *Odyssey* is full of eerie monsters and bizarre sorceries; they work in the same tradition as the unknown and much earlier author of the Mesopotamian Gilgamesh legend, that marvelous tale of the man who went seeking the secret of immortality; they supply, for a world much in need of such things, the glow and magic of the unfamiliar and extraordinary.

This book offers, without apology, escape into nine realms of the imagination, into lost worlds and unknown horizons of the mind, into dreams and hallucinations and eeriness. Some science fiction is terribly earnest about analyzing the flaws of society, and some is terribly earnest about predicting the coming developments in computers or organ-transplant techniques, and those are worthwhile and valid kinds of science fiction, but you will not find stories of that sort here. Here, just for once, is science fiction meant chiefly to amuse, divert, delight, and transport. These stories have no more social significance than the ones told by Scheherazade in *The Thousand and One Nights*—but those stories have given pleasure for a thousand and one years. Perhaps some of these may do so too.

—Robert Silverberg

LOST WORLDS, UNKNOWN HORIZONS

The Country of the Blind

H. G. WELLS

Herbert George Wells (1866-1946) was a man of many facets—historian, social critic, novelist—but he is best remembered today for the immortal science fiction that he produced in a ten-year span around the turn of the century. With such works as The War of the Worlds, The Time Machine, *and* The Island of Dr. Moreau, *he established standards by which all later science fiction must be judged. Many of his short stories deal with fantastic adventure in extraordinary places, and all are exciting and vivid, but of them all I think the famed "Country of the Blind" offers the richest insights into human nature and the most intense experience of the utterly strange.*

Three hundred miles and more from Chimborazo, one hundred from the snows of Cotopaxi, in the wildest wastes of Ecuador's Andes, there lies that mysterious mountain valley, cut off from the world of men, the Country of the Blind. Long years ago that valley lay so far open to the world that men might come at last through frightful gorges and over an icy pass into its equable meadows; and thither indeed men came, a family or so of Peruvian half-breeds fleeing from the lust and tyranny of an evil Spanish ruler. Then came the stupendous outbreak of Mindobamba, when it was night in Quito for seventeen days, and the water was boiling at Yaguachi and all the fish floating dying even as far as Guayaquil; everywhere along the Pacific slopes there were landslips and swift thawings and sudden floods, and one whole side of the old Arauca crest slipped and came down in thunder, and cut off the Country of the Blind for ever from the exploring feet of men. But one of these early settlers had chanced to be on the hither side of the gorges when the world had so terribly shaken itself, and he perforce had to forget his wife and his child and all the friends and possessions he had left up there, and start life over again in the lower world. He started it again but ill, blindness overtook him, and he died of punishment in the mines; but the story he told begot a legend that lingers along the length of the Cordilleras of the Andes to this day.

He told of his reason for venturing back from that fastness, into which he had first been carried lashed to a llama, beside a vast bale of gear, when he was a child. The valley, he said, had in it all that the heart of man could desire—sweet water, pasture, an even climate, slopes of rich brown soil with tangles of a shrub that bore an excellent fruit, and on one side great hanging forests of pine that held the avalanches high. Far overhead, on three sides, vast cliffs of grey-green rock were capped by cliffs of ice; but the glacier stream came not to them but flowed away by the farther slopes, and only now and then huge ice masses fell on the valley side. In this valley it neither rained nor snowed, but the abundant springs gave a rich green pasture, that irrigation would spread over all the valley space. The settlers did well indeed there. Their beasts did well and multiplied, and but one thing marred their happiness. Yet it was enough to mar it greatly. A strange disease had come upon them, and had made all the children born to them there—and indeed, several older children also—blind. It was to seek some charm or antidote against this plague of blindness that he had with fatigue and danger and difficulty returned down the gorge. In those days, in such cases, men did not think of germs and infections but of sins; and it seemed to him that the reason of this affliction must lie in the negligence of these priestless immigrants to set up a shrine so soon as they entered the valley. He wanted a shrine—a handsome, cheap, effectual shrine—to be erected in the valley; he wanted relics and such-like potent things of faith, blessed objects and mysterious medals and prayers. In his wallet he had a bar of native silver for which he would not account; he insisted there was none in the valley with something of the insistence of an inexpert liar. They had all clubbed their money and ornaments together, having little need for such treasure up there, he said, to buy them holy help against their ill. I figure this dim-eyed young mountaineer, sunburnt, gaunt, and anxious, hat-brim clutched feverishly, a man all unused to the ways of the lower world, telling this story to some keen-eyed, attentive priest before the great convulsion; I can picture him presently seeking to return with pious and infallible remedies against that trouble, and the infinite dismay with which he must have faced the tumbled vastness where the gorge had once come out. But the rest of his story of mischances is lost to me, save that I know of his evil death after several years. Poor stray from that remoteness! The stream that had once made the gorge now bursts from the mouth of a rocky cave, and the legend his poor, ill-told story set going developed into the legend of a race of blind men somewhere "over there" one may still hear to-day.

And amidst the little population of that now isolated and forgotten valley the disease ran its course. The old became groping and purblind, the young saw but dimly, and the children that were born to them saw never at all. But life was very easy in that snow-rimmed basin, lost to all the world, with neither thorns nor briars, with no evil insects nor any beasts save the gentle breed of llamas they had lugged and thrust and followed up the beds of the shrunken rivers in the gorges up which they had come. The seeing had become purblind so gradually that they scarcely noticed their loss. They guided the sightless youngsters hither and thither until they knew the whole valley marvellously, and when at last sight died out among them the race lived on. They had even time to adapt themselves to the blind control of fire, which they made carefully in stoves of stone. They were a simple strain of people at the first, unlettered, only slightly touched with the Spanish civilisation, but with something of a tradition of the arts of old Peru and of its lost philosophy. Generation followed generation. They forgot many things; they devised many things. Their tradition of the greater world they came from became mythical in colour and uncertain. In all things save sight they were strong and able; and presently the chance of birth and heredity sent one who had an original mind and who could talk and persuade among them, and then afterwards another. These two passed, leaving their effects, and the little community grew in numbers and in understanding, and met and settled social and economic problems that arose. Generation followed generation. There came a time when a child was born who was fifteen generations from that ancestor who went out of the valley with a bar of silver to seek God's aid, and who never returned. Thereabouts it chanced that a man came into this community from the outer world. And this is the story of that man.

He was a mountaineer from the country near Quito, a man who had been down to the sea and seen the world, a reader of books in an original way, an acute and enterprising man, and he was taken on by a party of Englishmen who had come out to Ecuador to climb mountains, to replace one of their three Swiss guides who had fallen ill. He climbed here and he climbed there, and then came the attempt on Parascotopetl, the Matterhorn of the Andes, in which he was lost to the outer world. The story of the accident has been written a dozen times. Pointer's narrative is the best. He tells how the party worked their difficult and almost vertical way up to the very foot of the last and greatest precipice, and how they built a night shelter amidst the snow upon a little shelf of rock, and, with a touch of real dramatic power, how presently they found Nuñez had gone from them. They shouted, and there was no reply; shouted and whistled, and for the rest of that night they slept no more.

As the morning broke they saw the traces of his fall. It seems impossible he could have uttered a sound. He had slipped eastward towards the unknown side of the mountain; far below he had struck a steep slope of snow, and ploughed his way down it in the midst of a snow avalanche. His track went straight to the edge of a frightful precipice, and beyond that everything was hidden. Far, far below, and hazy with distance, they could see trees rising out of a narrow, shut-in valley—the lost Country of the Blind. But they did not know it was the lost Country of the Blind, nor distinguish it in any way from any other narrow streak of upland valley. Unnerved by this disaster, they abandoned their attempt in the afternoon, and Pointer was called away to the war before he could make another attack. To this day Parascotopetl lifts an unconquered crest, and Pointer's shelter crumbles unvisited amidst the snows.

And the man who fell survived.

At the end of the slope he fell a thousand feet, and came down in the midst of a cloud of snow upon a snow slope even steeper than the one above. Down this he was whirled, stunned and insensible, but without a bone broken in his body; and then at last came to gentler slopes, and at last rolled out and lay still, buried amidst a softening heap of the white masses that had accompanied and saved him. He came to himself with a dim fancy that he was ill in bed; then realised his position with a mountaineer's intelligence, and worked himself loose, and after a rest or so, out until he saw the stars. He rested flat upon his chest for a space, wondering where he was and what had happened to him. He explored his limbs, and discovered that several of his buttons were gone and his coat turned over his head. His knife had gone from his pocket and his hat was lost, though he had tied it under his chin. He recalled that he had been looking for loose stones to raise his piece of the shelter wall. His ice-axe had disappeared.

He decided that he must have fallen, and looked up to see, exaggerated by the ghastly light of the rising moon, the tremendous flight he had taken. For a while he lay, gazing blankly at that vast pale cliff towering above, rising moment by moment out of a subsiding tide of darkness. Its phantasmal mysterious beauty held him for a space, and then he was seized with a paroxysm of sobbing laughter. . . .

After a great interval of time he became aware that he was near the lower edge of the snow. Below, down what was now a moonlit and practicable slope, he saw the dark and broken appearance of rock-strewn turf. He struggled to his feet, aching in every joint and limb, got down painfully from the heaped loose snow about him, went downward until he was on the turf, and there dropped rather than lay beside a boulder, drank deep from the flask in his inner pocket, and instantly fell asleep. . . .

He was awakened by the singing of birds in the trees far below.

He sat up and perceived he was on a little alp at the foot of a vast precipice, that was grooved by the gully down which he and his snow had come. Over against him another wall of rock reared itself against the sky. The gorge between these precipices ran east and west and was full of the morning sunlight, which lit to the westward the mass of fallen mountain that closed the descending gorge. Below him it seemed there was a precipice equally steep, but behind the snow in the gully he found a sort of chimney-cleft dripping with snow-water down which a desperate man might venture. He found it easier than it seemed, and came at last to another desolate alp, and then after a rock climb of no particular difficulty to a steep slope of trees. He took his bearings and turned his face up the gorge, for he saw it opened out above upon green meadows, among which he now glimpsed quite distinctly a cluster of stone huts of unfamiliar fashion. At times his progress was like clambering along the face of a wall, and after a time the rising sun ceased to strike along the gorge, the voices of the singing birds died away, and the air grew cold and dark about him. But the distant valley with its houses was all the brighter for that. He presently came to talus, and among the rocks he noted—for he was an observant man—an unfamiliar fern that seemed to clutch out of the crevices with intense green hands. He picked a frond or so and gnawed its stalk and found it helpful.

About midday he came at last out of the throat of the gorge into the plain and the sunlight. He was stiff and weary; he sat down in the shadow of a rock, filled up his flask with water from a spring and drank it down, and remained for a time resting before he went on to the houses.

They were very strange to his eyes, and indeed the whole aspect of that valley became, as he regarded it, queerer and more unfamiliar. The greater part of its surface was lush green meadow, starred with many beautiful flowers, irrigated with extraordinary care, and bearing evidence of systematic cropping piece by piece. High up and ringing the valley about was a wall, and what appeared to be a circumferential water-channel, from which the little trickles of water that fed the meadow plants came, and on the higher slopes above this flocks of llamas cropped the scanty herbage. Sheds, apparently shelters or feeding-places for the llamas, stood against the boundary wall here and there. The irrigation streams ran together into a main channel down the centre of the valley, and this was enclosed on either side by a wall breast high. This gave a singularly urban quality to this secluded place, a quality that was greatly enhanced by the fact that a number of paths paved with black and white stones, and each with a curious little kerb at the side, ran hither and thither in an orderly manner. The houses of the central village were quite unlike the casual and higgledy-piggledy agglomeration of the mountain villages he knew; they stood in a continuous row on either side of a central street of astonishing cleanness; here and there their parti-colored facade was pierced by a door, and not a solitary window broke their even frontage. They were parti-coloured with extraordinary irregularity; smeared with a sort of plaster that was sometimes grey, sometimes drab, sometimes slate-colored or dark brown;

and it was the sight of this wild plastering first brought the word "blind" into the thoughts of the explorer. "The good man who did that," he thought, "must have been as blind as a bat."

He descended a steep place, and so came to the wall and channel that ran about the valley, near where the latter spouted out its surplus contents into the deeps of the gorge in a thin and wavering thread of cascade. He could now see a number of men and women resting on piled heaps of grass, as if taking a siesta, in the remoter part of the meadow, and nearer the village a number of recumbent children, and then nearer at hand three men carrying pails on yokes along a little path that ran from the encircling wall towards the houses. These latter were clad in garments of llama cloth and boots and belts of leather, and they wore caps of cloth with back and ear flaps. They followed one another in single file, walking slowly and yawning as they walked, like men who have been up all night. There was something so reassuringly prosperous and respectable in their bearing that after a moment's hesitation Nuñez stood forward as conspicuously as possible upon his rock, and gave vent to a mighty shout that echoed round the valley.

The three men stopped, and moved their heads as though they were looking about them. They turned their faces this way and that, and Nuñez gesticulated with freedom. But they did not appear to see him for all his gestures, and after a time, directing themselves towards the mountains far away to the right, they shouted as if in answer. Nuñez bawled again, and then once more, and as he gestured ineffectually the word "blind" came up to the top of his thoughts. "These fools must be blind," he said.

When at last, after much shouting and wrath, Nuñez crossed the stream by a little bridge, came through a gate in the wall, and approached them, he was sure that they were blind. He was sure that this was the Country of the Blind of which the legends told. Conviction had sprung upon him, and a sense of great and rather enviable adventure. The three stood side by side, not looking at him, but with their ears directed towards him, judging him by

THE COUNTRY OF THE BLIND

his unfamiliar steps. They stood close together like men a little afraid, and he could see their eyelids closed and sunken, as though the very balls beneath had shrunk away. There was an expression near awe on their faces.

"A man," one said, in hardly recognisable Spanish— "a man it is—a man or a spirit—coming down from the rocks."

But Nuñez advanced with the confident steps of a youth who enters upon life. All the old stories of the lost valley and the Country of the Blind had come back to his mind, and through his thoughts ran this old proverb, as if it were a refrain—

"In the Country of the Blind the One-eyed Man is King."

"In the Country of the Blind the One-eyed Man is King."

And very civilly he gave them greeting. He talked to them and used his eyes.

"Where does he come from, brother Pedro?" asked one.

"Down out of the rocks."

"Over the mountains I come," said Nuñez, "out of the country beyond there—where men can see. From near Bogotá, where there are a hundred thousands of people, and where the city passes out of sight."

"Sight?" muttered Pedro. "Sight?"

"He comes," said the second blind man, "out of the rocks."

The cloth of their coats, Nuñez saw, was curiously fashioned, each with a different sort of stitching.

They startled him by a simultaneous movement towards him, each with a hand outstretched. He stepped back from the advance of those spread fingers.

"Come hither," said the third blind man, following his motion and clutching him neatly.

And they held Nuñez and felt him over, saying no word further until they had done so.

"Carefully," he cried, with a finger in his eye, and found they thought that organ, with its fluttering lids, a queer thing in him. They went over it again.

"A strange creature, Correa," said the one called Pedro. "Feel the coarseness of his hair. Like a llama's hair."

"Rough he is as the rocks that begot him," said Correa, investigating Nuñez's unshaven chin with a soft and slightly moist hand. "Perhaps he will grow finer." Nuñez struggled a little under their examination, but they gripped him firm.

"Carefully," he said again.

"He speaks," said the third man. "Certainly he is a man."

"Ugh!" said Pedro, at the roughness of his coat.

"And you have come into the world?" asked Pedro.

"*Out* of the world. Over mountains and glaciers; right over above there, halfway to the sun. Out of the great big world that goes down, twelve days' journey to the sea."

They scarcely seemed to heed him. "Our fathers have told us men may be made by the forces of Nature," said Correa. "It is the warmth of things and moisture, and rottenness—rottenness."

"Let us lead him to the elders," said Pedro.

"Shout first," said Correa, "lest the children be afraid. This is a marvellous occasion."

So they shouted, and Pedro went first and took Nuñez by the hand to lead him to the houses.

He drew his hand away. "I can see," he said.

"See?" said Correa.

"Yes, see," said Nuñez, turning towards him, and stumbled against Pedro's pail.

"His senses are still imperfect," said the third blind man. "He stumbles, and talks unmeaning words. Lead him by the hand."

"As you will," said Nuñez, and was led along, laughing.

It seemed they knew nothing of sight.

Well, all in good time he would teach them.

He heard people shouting, and saw a number of figures gathering together in the middle roadway of the village.

He found it tax his nerve and patience more than he had anticipated, that first encounter with the population of the Country of the Blind. The place seemed larger as he drew near to it, and the smeared plasterings queerer, and a crowd of children and men and women (the women and girls, he was pleased to note, had some of them quite sweet faces, for all that their eyes were shut and sunken) came about him, holding on to him, touching him with soft, sensitive hands, smelling at him, and listening to every word he spoke. Some of the maidens and children, however, kept aloof as if afraid, and indeed his voice seemed coarse and rude beside their softer notes. They mobbed him. His three guides kept close to him with an effect of proprietorship, and said again and again, "A wild man out of the rocks."

"Bogotá," he said. "Bogotá. Over the mountain crests."

"A wild man—using wild words," said Pedro. "Did you hear that—*Bogotá?* His mind is hardly formed yet. He has only the beginnings of speech."

A little boy nipped his hand. "Bogotá," he said mockingly.

"Ay! A city to your village. I come from the great world—where men have eyes and see."

"His name's Bogotá," they said.

"He stumbled," said Correa, "stumbled twice as we came hither."

"Bring him to the elders."

And they thrust him suddenly through a doorway into a room as black as pitch, save at the end there faintly glowed a fire. The crowd closed in behind him and shut out all but the faintest glimmer of day, and before he could arrest himself he had fallen headlong over the feet of a seated man. His arm, out-flung, struck the face of someone else as he went down; he felt the soft impact of features and heard a cry of anger, and for a moment he struggled against a number of hands that clutched him. It was a one-sided fight. An inkling of the situation came to him, and he lay quiet.

"I fell down," he said; "I couldn't see in this pitchy darkness."

There was a pause as if the unseen persons about him tried to understand his words. Then the voice of Correa said: "He is but newly formed. He stumbles as he walks and mingles words that mean nothing with his speech."

Others also said things about him that he heard or understood imperfectly.

"May I sit up?" he asked, in a pause. "I will not struggle against you again."

They consulted and let him rise.

The voice of an older man began to question him, and Nuñez found himself trying to explain the great world out of which he had fallen, and the sky and mountains and sight and such-like marvels, to these elders who sat in darkness in the Country of the Blind. And they would believe and understand nothing whatever he told them, a thing quite outside his expectation. They would not even understand many of his words. For fourteen generations these people had been blind and cut off from all the seeing world; the names for all the things of sight had faded and changed to a child's story; and they had ceased to concern themselves with anything beyond the rocky slopes above their circling wall. Blind men of genius had arisen among them and questioned the shreds of belief and tradition they had brought with them from their seeing days, and had dismissed all these things as idle fancies, and replaced them with new and saner explanations. Much of their imagination had shrivelled with their eyes, and they had made for themselves new imaginations with their ever more sensitive ears and fingertips. Slowly Nuñez realised this; that his expectation of wonder and reverence at his origin and his gifts was not to be borne out; and after his poor attempt to explain sight to them had been set aside as the confused version of a new-made being describing the marvels of his incoherent sensations, he subsided, a little dashed, into listening to their instruction. And the eldest of the blind men explained to him life and philosophy and religion, how that the world (meaning their valley) had been first an empty hollow in the rocks, and then had come, first, inanimate things without the gift of touch, and llamas and a few other creatures that had little sense, and then men, and at last angels, whom one could hear singing and making fluttering sounds, but whom no one could touch at all, which puzzled Nuñez greatly until he thought of the birds.

He went on to tell Nuñez how this time had been divided into the warm and the cold, which are the blind equivalents of day and night, and how it was good to sleep in the warm and work during the cold, so that now, but for his advent, the whole town of the blind would have been asleep. He said Nuñez must have been specially created to learn and serve the wisdom they had acquired, and for that all his mental incoherency and stumbling behavior he must have courage and do his best to learn, and at that all the people in the doorway murmured encouragingly. He said the night—for the blind call their day night—was now far gone, and it behooved everyone to go back to sleep. He asked Nuñez if he knew how to sleep, and Nuñez said he did, but that before sleep he wanted food.

They brought him food—llama's milk in a bowl, and rough salted bread—and led him into a lonely place to eat out of their hearing, and afterwards to slumber until the chill of the mountain evening roused them to begin their day again. But Nuñez slumbered not at all.

Instead, he sat in the place where they had left him, resting his limbs and turning the unanticipated circumstances of his arrival over and over in his mind.

Every now and then he laughed, sometimes with amusement, and sometimes with indignation.

"Unformed mind!" he said. "Got no sense yet! They little know they've been insulting their heaven-sent king and master. I see I must bring them to reason. Let me think—let me think."

He was still thinking when the sun set.

Nuñez had an eye for all beautiful things, and it seemed to him that the glow upon the snowfields and glaciers that rose about the valley on every side was the most beautiful thing he had ever seen. His eyes went from that inaccessible glory to the village and irrigated fields, fast sinking into the twilight, and suddenly a wave of emotion took him, and he thanked God from the bottom of his heart that the power of sight had been given him.

He heard a voice calling to him from out of the village.

"Ya ho there, Bogotá! Come hither!"

At that he stood up smiling. He would show these people once and for all what sight would do for a man. They would seek him, but not find him.

"You move not, Bogotá," said the voice.

He laughed noiselessly, and made two stealthy steps aside from the path.

"Trample not on the grass, Bogotá; that is not allowed."

Nuñez had scarcely heard the sound he made himself. He stopped, amazed.

The owner of the voice came running up the piebald path towards him.

He stepped back into the pathway. "Here I am," he said.

"Why did you not come when I called you?" said the blind man. "Must you be led like a child? Cannot you hear the path as you walk?"

Nuñez laughed. "I can see it," he said.

"There is no such word as *see*," said the blind man, after a pause. "Cease this folly, and follow the sound of my feet."

Nuñez followed, a little annoyed.

"My time will come," he said.

"You'll learn," the blind man answered. "There is much to learn in the world."

"Has no one told you, 'In the Country of the Blind the One-eyed Man is King'?"

"What is blind?" asked the blind man carelessly over his shoulder.

Four days passed, and the fifth found the King of the Blind still incognito, as a clumsy and useless stranger among his subjects.

It was, he found, much more difficult to proclaim himself than he had supposed, and in the meantime, while he meditated his *coup d'état*, he did what he was told and learned the manners and customs of the Country of the Blind. He found working and going about at night a particularly irksome thing, and he decided that that should be the first thing he would change.

They led a simple, laborious life, these people, with all the elements of virtue and happiness, as these things can be understood by men. They toiled, but not oppressively; they had food and clothing sufficient for their needs; they had days and seasons of rest; they made much of music and singing, and there was love among them, and little children.

It was marvellous with what confidence and precision they went about their ordered world. Everything, you see, had been made to fit their needs; each of the radiating paths of the valley area had a constant angle to the others, and was distinguished by a special notch upon its kerbing; all obstacles and irregularities of path or meadow had long since been cleared away; all their methods and procedure arose naturally from their special needs. Their senses had become marvellously acute; they could hear and judge the slightest gesture of a man a dozen paces away—could hear the very beating of his heart. Intonation had long replaced expression with them, and touches gesture, and their work with hoe and spade and fork was as free and confident as garden work can be. Their sense of smell was extraordinarily fine; they could distinguish individual differences as readily as a dog can, and they went about the tending of the llamas, who lived among the rocks above and came to the wall for food and shelter, with ease and confidence. It was only when at last Nuñez sought to assert himself that he found how easy and confident their movements could be.

He rebelled only after he had tried persuasion.

He tried at first on several occasions to tell them of sight. "Look you here, you people." he said. "There are things you do not understand in me."

Once or twice one or two of them attended to him; they sat with faces downcast and ears turned intelligently towards him, and he did his best to tell them what it was to see. Among his hearers was a girl, with eyelids less red and sunken than the others, so that one could almost fancy she was hiding eyes, whom especially he hoped to persuade. He spoke of the beauties of sight, of watching the mountains, of the sky and the sunrise, and they heard him with amused incredulity that presently became condemnatory. They told him there were indeed no mountains at all, but that the end of the rocks where the llamas grazed was indeed the end of the world; thence sprang a cavernous roof of the universe, from which the dew and the avalanches fell; and when he maintained stoutly the world had neither end nor roof such as they supposed, they said his thoughts were wicked. So far as he could describe sky and clouds and stars to them it seemed to them a hideous void, a terrible blankness in the place of the smooth roof to things in which they believed—it was an article of faith with them that the cavern roof was exquisitely smooth to the touch. He saw that in some manner he shocked them, and gave up that aspect of the matter altogether, and tried to show them the practical value of sight. One morning he saw Pedro in the path called Seventeen and coming towards the central houses, but still too far off for hearing or scent, and he told them as much. "In a little while," he prophesied, "Pedro will be here." An old man remarked that Pedro had no business on Path Seventeen, and then, as if in confirmation, that individual as he drew near turned and went transversely into Path Ten, and so back with nimble paces towards the outer wall. They mocked Nuñez when Pedro did not arrive, and afterwards, when he asked Pedro questions to clear his character, Pedro denied and outfaced him, and was afterwards hostile to him.

Then he induced them to let him go a long way up the sloping meadows towards the wall with one complacent individual, and to him he promised to describe all that happened among the houses. He noted certain goings and comings, but the things that really seemed to signify to these people happened inside of or behind the windowless houses—the only things they took note of to test him by—and of these he could see or tell nothing; and it was after the failure of this attempt, and the ridicule they could not repress, that he resorted to force. He thought of seizing a spade and suddenly smiting one or two of them to earth, and so in fair combat showing the advantage of eyes. He went so far with that resolution as to seize his spade, and then he discovered a new thing about himself, and that was that it was impossible for him to hit a blind man in cold blood.

He hesitated, and found them all aware that he had snatched up the spade. They stood alert, with their heads on one side, and bent ears towards him for what he would do next.

"Put that spade down," said one, and he felt a sort of helpless horror. He came near obedience.

Then he thrust one backwards against a house wall, and fled past him and out of the village.

He went athwart one of their meadows, leaving a track of trampled grass behind his feet, and presently sat down by the side of one of their ways. He felt something of the buoyancy that comes to all men in the beginning of a fight, but more perplexity. He began to realise that you cannot even fight happily with creatures who stand upon a different mental basis to yourself. Far away he saw a number of men carrying spades and sticks come out of the street of houses, and advance in a spreading line along the several paths towards him. They advanced slowly, speaking frequently to one another, and ever and again the whole cordon would halt and sniff the air and listen.

The first time they did this Nuñez laughed. But afterwards he did not laugh.

One struck his trail in the meadow grass, and came stooping and feeling his way along it.

For five minutes he watched the slow extension of the cordon, and then his vague disposition to do something forthwith became frantic. He stood up, went a pace or two towards the circumferential wall, turned, and went back a little way.

There they all stood in a crescent, still and listening.

He also stood still, gripping his space very tightly in both hands. Should he charge them?

The pulse in his ears ran into the rhythm of "In the Country of the Blind the One-eyed Man is King!"

Should he charge them?

He looked back at the high and unclimbable wall behind— unclimbable because of its smooth plastering, but withal pierced with many little doors, and at the approaching line of seekers. Behind these, others were now coming out of the street of houses.

Should he charge them?

"Bogotá!" called one. "Bogotá! Where are you?"

He gripped his spade still tighter, and advanced down the meadows towards the place of habitations, and directly he moved they converged upon him. "I'll hit them if they touch me," he swore; "by Heaven, I will. I'll hit." He called aloud, "Look here, I'm going to do what I like in this valley. Do you hear? I'm going to do what I like and go where I like!"

They were moving in upon him quickly, groping, yet moving rapidly. It was like playing blind man's buff, with everyone blindfolded except one. "Get hold of him!" cried one. He found himself in the arc of a loose curve of pursuers. He felt suddenly he must be active and resolute.

"You don't understand," he cried in a voice that was meant to be great and resolute, and which broke. "You are blind, and I can see. Leave me alone!"

"Bogotá! Put down that spade, and come off the grass!"

The last order, grotesque in its urban familiarity, produced a gust of anger.

"I'll hurt you," he said, sobbing with emotion. "By Heaven, I'll hurt you. Leave me alone!"

He began to run, not knowing clearly where to run. He ran from the nearest blind man, because it was a horror to hit him. He stopped, and then made a dash to escape from their closing ranks. He made for where a gap was wide, and the men on either side, with a quick perception of the approach of his paces, rushed in on one another. He sprang forward, and then saw he must be caught, and *swish!* the spade had struck. He felt the soft thud of hand and arm, and the man was down with a yell of pain, and he was through.

Through! And then he was close to the street of houses again, and blind men, whirling spades and stakes, were running with a sort of reasoned swiftness hither and thither.

He heard steps behind him just in time, and found a tall man rushing foward and swiping at the sound of him. He lost his nerve, hurled his spade a yard wide at his antagonist, and whirled about and fled, fairly yelling as he dodged another.

He was panic-stricken. He ran furiously to and fro, dodging when there was no need to dodge, and in his anxiety to see on every side of him at once, stumbling. For a moment he was down and they heard his fall. Far away in the circumferential wall a little doorway looked like heaven, and he set off in a wild rush for it. He did not even look round at his pursuers until it was gained, and he had stumbled across the bridge, clambered a little way among the rocks, to the surprise and dismay of a young llama, who went leaping out of sight, and lay down sobbing for breath.

And so his *coup d'état* came to an end.

He stayed outside the wall of the valley of the Blind for two nights and days without food or shelter, and meditated upon the unexpected. During these meditations he repeated very frequently and always with a profounder note of derision the exploded proverb: "In the Country of the Blind the One-eyed Man is King." He thought chiefly of ways of fighting and conquering these people, and it grew clearer that for him no practicable way was possible. He had no weapons, and now it would be hard to get one.

The canker of civilisation had got to him even in Bogotá, and he could not find it in himself to go down and assassinate a blind man. Of course, if he did that, he might then dictate terms on the threat of assassinating them all. But—sooner or later he must sleep!

He tried also to find food among the pine trees, to be comfortable under pine boughs while the frost fell at night, and—with less confidence—to catch a llama by artifice in order to try to kill it—perhaps by hammering it with a stone—and so, finally, perhaps, to eat some of it. But the llamas had a doubt of him and regarded him with distrustful brown eyes, and spat when he drew near. Fear came on him the second day and fits of shivering. Finally he crawled down to the wall of the Country of the Blind and tried to make terms. He crawled along by the stream, shouting, until two blind men came to the gate and talked to him.

"I was mad," he said. "But I was only newly made."

They said that was better.

He told them he was wiser now, and repented of all he had done.

Then he wept without intention, for he was very weak and ill now, and they took that as a favourable sign.

They asked him if he still thought he could "*see*."

"No," he said. "That was folly. The word means nothing—less than nothing!"

They asked him what was overhead.

"About ten times ten the height of a man there is a roof above the world—of rock—and very, very smooth." He burst again into hysterical tears. "Before you ask me any more, give me some food or I shall die."

He expected dire punishments, but these blind people were capable of toleration. They regarded his rebellion as but one more proof of his general idiocy and inferiority; and after they had whipped him they appointed him to do the simplest and heaviest work they had for anyone to do, and he, seeing no other way of living, did submissively what he was told.

He was ill for some days, and they nursed him kindly. That refined his submission. But they insisted on his lying in the

THE COUNTRY OF THE BLIND

dark, and that was a great misery. And blind philosophers came and talked to him of the wicked levity of his mind, and reproved him so impressively for his own doubts about the lid of rock that covered their cosmic casserole that he almost doubted whether indeed he was not the victim of hallucination in not seeing it overhead.

So Nuñez became a citizen of the Country of the Blind, and these people ceased to be a generalised people and became individualities and familiar to him, while the world beyond the mountains became more and more remote and unreal. There was Yacob, his master, a kindly man when not annoyed; there was Pedro, Yacob's nephew; and there was Medina-sarote, who was the youngest daughter of Yacob. She was little esteemed in the world of the Blind, because she had a clear-cut face, and lacked that satisfying, glossy smoothness that is the blind man's ideal of feminine beauty; but Nuñez thought her beautiful at first, and presently the most beautiful thing in the whole creation. Her closed eyelids were not sunken and red after the common way of the valley, but lay as though they might open again at any moment; and she had long eyelashes, which were considered a grave disfigurement. And her voice was strong, and did not satisfy the acute hearing of the valley swains. So that she had no lover.

There came a time when Nuñez thought that, could he win her, he would be resigned to live in the valley for all the rest of his days.

He watched her; he sought opportunities for doing her little services, and presently he found that she observed him. Once at a rest-day gathering they sat side by side in the dim starlight, and the music was sweet. His hand came upon hers and he dared to clasp it. Then very tenderly she returned his pressure. And one day, as they were at their meal in the darkness, he felt her hand very softly seeking him, and as it chanced the fire leaped then and he saw the tenderness of her face.

He sought to speak to her.

He went to her one day when she was sitting in the summer

moonlight spinning. The light made her a thing of silver and mystery. He sat down at her feet and told her that he loved her, and told her how beautiful she seemed to him. He had a lover's voice, he spoke with a tender reverence that came near to awe, and she had never before been touched by adoration. She made him no definite answer, but it was clear that his words pleased her.

After that he talked to her whenever he could take an opportunity. The valley became the world for him, and the world beyond the mountains where men lived in sunlight seemed no more than a fairy tale he would some day pour into her ears. Very tentatively and timidly he spoke to her of sight.

Sight seemed to her the most poetical of fancies, and she listened to his description of the stars and the mountains and her own sweet white-lit beauty as though it were a guilty indulgence. She did not believe, she could only half understand, but she was mysteriously delighted, and it seemed to him that she completely understood.

His love lost its awe and took courage. Presently he was for demanding her of Yacob and the elders in marriage, but she became fearful and delayed. And it was one of her elder sisters who first told Yacob that Medina-sarote and Nuñez were in love.

There was from the first very great opposition to the marriage of Nuñez and Medina-sarote; not so much because they valued her as because they held him as a being apart, an idiot, incompetent thing below the permissible level of a man. Her sisters opposed it bitterly as bringing discredit on them all; and old Yacob, though he had formed a sort of liking for his clumsy, obedient serf, shook his head and said the thing could not be. The young men were all angry at the idea of corrupting the race, and one went so far as to revile and strike Nuñez. He struck back. Then for the first time he found an advantage in seeing, even by twilight, and after that fight no one was disposed to raise a hand against him. But they still found his marriage impossible.

Old Yacob had a tenderness for his last little daughter, and was grieved to have her weep upon his shoulder.

"You see, my dear, he's an idiot. He has delusions; he can't do anything right."

"I know," wept Medina-sarote. "But he's better than he was. He's getting better. And he's strong, dear father, and kind—stronger and kinder than any other man in the world. And he loves me—and, Father, I love him."

Old Yacob was greatly distressed to find her inconsolable, and besides—what made it more distressing—he liked Nuñez for many things. So he went and sat in the windowless council-chamber with the other elders, and watched the trend of the talk, and said, at the proper time, "He's better than he was. Very likely, some day, we shall find him as ourselves."

Then afterwards one of the elders, who thought deeply, had an idea. He was the great doctor among these people, their medicine-man, and he had a very philosophical and inventive mind, and the idea of curing Nuñez of his peculiarities appealed to him. One day when Yacob was present he returned to the topic of Nuñez.

"I have examined Bogotá," he said, "and the case is clearer to me. I think very probably he might be cured."

"That is what I have always hoped," said old Yacob.

"His brain is affected," said the blind doctor.

The elders murmured assent.

"Now, *what* affects it?"

"Ah!" said old Yacob.

"*This*," said the doctor, answering his own question. "Those queer things that are called the eyes, and which exist to make an agreeable soft depression in the face, are diseased, in the case of Bogotá, in such a way as to affect his brain. They are greatly distended, he has eyelashes, and his eyelids move, and consequently his brain is in a state of constant irritation and distraction."

"Yes?" said old Yacob. "Yes?"

"And I think I may say with reasonable certainty that, in

order to cure him completely, all that we need do is a simple and easy surgical operation—namely, to remove these irritant bodies."

"And then he will be sane?"

"Then he will be perfectly sane, and a quite admirable citizen."

"Thank Heaven for science!" said old Yacob, and went forth at once to tell Nuñez of his happy hopes.

But Nuñez's manner of receiving the good news struck him as being cold and disappointing.

"One might think," he said, "from the tone you take, that you did not care for my daughter."

It was Medina-sarote who persuaded Nuñez to face the blind surgeons.

"*You* do not want me," he said, "to lose my gift of sight?"

She shook her head.

"My world is sight."

Her head drooped lower.

"There are the beautiful things, the beautiful little things—the flowers, the lichens among the rocks, the lightness and softness of a piece of fur, the far sky with its drifting down of clouds, the sunsets and the stars. And there is *you*. For you alone it is good to have sight, to see your sweet, serene face, your kindly lips, your dear, beautiful hands folded together. . . . It is these eyes of mine you won, these eyes that hold me to you, that these idiots seek. Instead, I must touch you, hear you, and never see you again. I must come under that roof of rock and stone and darkness, that horrible roof under which your imagination stoops. . . . No; you would not have me do that?"

A disagreeable doubt had arisen in him. He stopped, and left the thing a question.

"I wish," she said, "sometimes—" She paused.

"Yes?" said he, a little apprehensively.

"I wish sometimes—you would not talk like that."

"Like what?"

"I know it's pretty—it's your imagination. I love it, but now—"

He felt cold. "*Now?*" he said faintly.

She sat still.

"You mean—you think—I should be better, better perhaps—"

He was realising things very swiftly. He felt anger, indeed, anger at the dull course of fate, but also sympathy for her lack of understanding—a sympathy near akin to pity.

"*Dear*," he said, and he could see by her whiteness how intensely her spirit pressed against the things she could not say. He put his arms about her, he kissed her ear, and they sat for a time in silence.

"If I were to consent to this?" he said at last, in a voice that was very gentle.

She flung her arms about him, weeping wildly. "Oh, if you would," she sobbed, "if only you would!"

For a week before the operation that was to raise him from his servitude and inferiority to the level of a blind citizen, Nuñez knew nothing of sleep, and all through the warm sunlit hours, while the others slumbered happily, he sat brooding or wandered aimlessly, trying to bring his mind to bear on his dilemma. He had given his answer, he had given his consent, and still he was not sure. And at last work-time was over, the sun rose in splendour over the golden crests, and his last day of vision began for him. He had a few minutes with Medina-sarote before she went apart to sleep.

"To-morrow," he said, "I shall see no more."

"Dear heart!" she answered, and pressed his hands with all her strength.

"They will hurt you but little," she said; "and you are going through this pain—you are going through it, dear lover, for *me*. . . . Dear, if a woman's heart and life can do it, I will repay you. My dearest one, my dearest with the tender voice, I will repay."

He was drenched in pity for himself and her.

He held her in his arms, and pressed his lips to hers, and looked on her sweet face for the last time. "Good-bye!" he whispered at that dear sight, "good-bye!"

And then in silence he turned away from her.

She could hear his slow retreating footsteps, and something in the rhythm of them threw her into a passion of weeping.

He had fully meant to go to a lonely place where the meadows were beautiful with white narcissus, and there remain until the hour of his sacrifice should come, but as he went he lifted up his eyes and saw the morning, the morning like an angel in golden armour, marching down the steeps. . . .

It seemed to him that before this splendour he, and this blind world in the valley, and his love, and all, were no more than a pit of sin.

He did not turn aside as he had meant to do, but went on, and passed through the wall of the circumference and out upon the rocks, and his eyes were always upon the sunlit ice and snow.

He saw their infinite beauty, and his imagination soared over them to the things beyond he was now to resign for ever.

He thought of the great free world he was parted from, the world that was his own, and he had a vision of those further slopes, distance beyond distance, with Bogotá, a place of multitudinous stirring beauty, a glory by day, a luminous mystery by night, a place of palaces and fountains and statues and white houses, lying beautifully in the middle distance. He thought how for a day or so one might come down through passes, drawing ever nearer and nearer to its busy streets and ways. He thought of the river journey, day by day, from great Bogotá to the still vaster world beyond, through towns and villages, forest and desert places, the rushing river day by day, until its banks receded and the big steamers came splashing by, and one had reached the sea—the limitless sea, with its thousand islands, its thousands of islands, and its ships seen dimly far away in their incessant journeyings round and about that greater world. And there, unpent by mountains, one saw the sky—the sky, not such a disc as one saw it here, but an arch of immeasurable blue, a deep of deeps in which the circling stars were floating. . . .

His eyes scrutinised the great curtain of the mountains with a keener inquiry.

For example, if one went so, up that gully and to that chimney there, then one might come out high among those stunted pines that ran round in a sort of shelf and rose still higher and higher as it passed above the gorge. And then? That talus might be managed. Thence perhaps a climb might be found to take him up to the precipice that came below the snow; and if that chimney failed, then another farther to the east might serve his purpose better. And then? Then one would be out upon the amber-lit snow there, and halfway up to the crest of those beautiful desolations.

He glanced back at the village, then turned right round and regarded it steadfastly.

He thought of Medina-sarote, and she had become small and remote.

He turned again towards the mountain wall, down which the day had come to him.

Then very circumspectly he began to climb.

When sunset came he was no longer climbing, but he was far and high. He had been higher, but he was still very high. His clothes were torn, his limbs were blood-stained, he was bruised in many places, but he lay as if he were at his ease, and there was a smile on his face.

From where he rested the valley seemed as if it were in a pit and nearly a mile below. Already it was dim with haze and shadow, though the mountain summits around him were things of light and fire. The little details of the rocks near at hand were drenched with a subtle beauty—a vein of green mineral piercing the grey, the flash of crystal faces here and there, a minute, minutely beautiful orange lichen close beside his face. There were deep mysterious shadows in the gorge, blue deepening into purple, and purple into a luminous darkness, and overhead was the illimitable vastness of the sky. But he heeded these things no longer, but lay quite inactive there, smiling as if he were satisfied merely to have escaped from the valley of the Blind in which he had thought to be King.

The glow of the sunset passed, and the night came, and still he lay peacefully contented under the cold stars.

The Third Level

JACK FINNEY

Every moment a mighty door swings shut on another segment of our past. The past is the great lost world; we can no more revisit yesterday than we can tour the London of Henry VIII or the bazaars of vanished Atlantis. And yet we return to the past in memory and in the reveries of fantasy. No writer has been more concerned with the irretrievability of the past than Jack Finney, as in the moving and ingenious novel Time and Again *and in such short stories as "Second Chance," "I'm Scared," and the delicious little "The Third Level" —in which yesterday is just around the four-dimensional corner.*

The presidents of the New York Central and the New York, New Haven, and Hartford railroads will swear on a stack of timetables that there are only two. But I say there are three, because I've *been* on the third level at Grand Central Station. Yes, I've taken the obvious step: I talked to a psychiatrist friend of mine, among others. I told him about the third level at Grand Central Station, and he said it was a waking-dream wish fulfillment. He said I was unhappy. That made my wife kind of mad, but he explained that he meant the modern world is full of insecurity, fear, war, worry, and all the rest of it, and that I just want to escape. Well, hell, who doesn't? Everybody I know wants to escape, but they don't wander down into any third level at Grand Central Station.

But that's the reason, he said, and my friends all agreed. Everything points to it, they claimed. My stamp collecting, for example—that's a "temporary refuge from reality." Well, maybe, but my grandfather didn't need any refuge from reality; things were pretty nice and peaceful in his day, from all I hear, and he started my collection. It's a nice collection, too, blocks of four of practically every United States issue, first-day covers, and so on. President Roosevelt collected stamps, too.

Anyway, here's what happened at Grand Central. One night last summer I worked late at the office. I was in a hurry to get uptown to my apartment, so I decided to subway from Grand Central because it's faster than the bus.

Now, I don't know why this should have happened to me. I'm just an ordinary guy named Charley, thirty-one years old, and I was wearing a tan gabardine suit and a straw hat with a fancy band—I passed a dozen men who looked just like me. And I wasn't trying to escape from anything; I just wanted to get home to Louisa, my wife.

I turned into Grand Central from Vanderbilt Avenue and went down the steps to the first level, where you take trains like the Twentieth Century. Then I walked down another flight to the second level, where the suburban trains leave from, ducked into an arched doorway headed for the subway—and got lost. That's easy to do. I've been in and out of Grand Central hundreds of times, but I'm always bumping into new doorways and stairs and corridors. Once I got into a tunnel about a mile long and came out in the lobby of the Roosevelt Hotel. Another time I came up in an office building on Forty-sixth Street, three blocks away.

Sometimes I think Grand Central is growing like a tree, pushing out new corridors and staircases like roots. There's probably a long tunnel that nobody knows about feeling its way

THE THIRD LEVEL

under the city right now, on its way to Times Square, and maybe another to Central Park. And maybe—because for so many people through the years Grand Central *has* been an exit, a way of escape—maybe that's how the tunnel I got into . . . but I never told my psychiatrist friend about that idea.

The corridor I was in began angling left and slanting downward and I thought that was wrong, but I kept on walking. All I could hear was the empty sound of my own footsteps and I didn't pass a soul. Then I heard that sort of hollow roar ahead that means open space, and people talking. The tunnel turned sharp left; I went down a short flight of stairs and came out on the third level at Grand Central Station. For just a moment I thought I was back on the second level, but I saw the room was smaller, there were fewer ticket windows and train gates, and the information booth in the center was wood and old-looking. And the man in the booth wore a green eyeshade and long black sleeve-protectors. The lights were dim and sort of flickering. Then I saw why: they were open-flame gaslights.

There were brass spittoons on the floor, and across the station a glint of light caught my eye: a man was pulling a gold watch from his vest pocket. He snapped open the cover, glanced at his watch, and frowned. He wore a dirty hat, a black four-button suit with tiny lapels, and he had a big, black, handle-bar mustache. Then I looked around and saw that everyone in the station was dressed like 1890 something; I never saw so many beards, sideburns and fancy mustaches in my life. A woman walked in through the train gate; she wore a dress with leg-of-mutton sleeves and skirts to the top of her high-buttoned shoes. Back of her, out on the tracks, I caught a glimpse of a locomotive, a very small Currier & Ives locomotive with a funnel-shaped stack. And then I knew.

To make sure, I walked over to a newsboy and glanced at the stack of papers at his feet. It was the *World;* and the *World* hasn't been published for years. The lead story said something about President Cleveland. I've found that front page since, in the Public Library files, and it was printed June 11, 1894.

I turned toward the ticket windows knowing that here—on the third level at Grand Central— I could buy tickets that would take Louisa and me anywhere in the United States we wanted to go. In the year 1894. And I wanted two tickets to Galesburg, Illinois.

Have you ever been there? It's a wonderful town still, with big old frame houses, huge lawns, and tremendous trees whose branches meet overhead and roof the streets. And in 1894, summer evenings were twice as long, and people sat out on their lawns, the men smoking cigars and talking quietly, the women waving palm-leaf fans, with the fireflies all around, in a peaceful world. To be back there with the First World War still twenty years off, and World War II over forty years in the future . . . I wanted two tickets for that.

The clerk checked the fare—he glanced at my fancy hatband, but he figured the fare—and I had enough for two coach tickets, one way. But when I counted out the money and looked up, the clerk was staring at me. He nodded at the bills. "That ain't money, mister," he said, "and if you're trying to skin me you won't get very far," and he glanced at the cash drawer beside him. Of course the money was old-style bills, half again as big as the money we use nowadays, and different-looking. I turned away and got out fast. There's nothing nice about jail, even in 1894.

And that was that. I left the same way I came, I suppose. Next day, during lunch hour, I drew $300 out of the bank, nearly all we had, and bought old-style currency (that *really* worried my psychiatrist friend). You can buy old money at almost any coin dealer's but you have to pay a premium. My $300 bought less than $200 in old-style bills, but I didn't care; eggs were thirteen cents a dozen in 1894.

But I've never again found the corridor that leads to the third level at Grand Central Station, although I've tried often enough.

Louisa was pretty worried when I told her all this and didn't want me to look for the third level any more, and after a while I stopped; I went back to my stamps. But now we're *both* looking, every weekend, because now we have proof that the third level is still there. My friend Sam Weiner disappeared! Nobody knew where, but I sort of suspected because Sam's a city boy, and I used to tell him about Galesburg—I went to school there—and he always said he liked the sound of the place. And that's where he is, all right. In 1894.

Because one night, fussing with my stamp collection, I found—well, do you know what a first-day cover is? When a new stamp is issued, stamp collectors buy some and use them to mail envelopes to themselves on the very first day of sale; and the postmark proves the date. The envelope is called a first-day envelope. They're never opened; you just put blank paper in the envelope.

That night, among my oldest first-day covers, I found one that shouldn't have been there. But there it was. It was there because someone had mailed it to my grandfather at his home in Galesburg; that's what the address on the envelope said. And it had been there since July 18, 1894—the postmark showed that—yet I didn't remember it at all. The stamp was a six-cent, dull brown, with a picture of President Garfield. Naturally, when the envelope came to Granddad in the mail, it went right into his collection and stayed there—till I took it out and opened it.

The paper inside wasn't blank. It read:

941 Willard Street
July 18, 1894
Galesburg, Illinois

Charley:

I got to wishing that you were right. Then I got to *believing* you were right. And, Charley, it's true: I found the third level! I've been here two weeks, and right now, down the street at the Daly's, someone is playing a piano, and they're all out on the front porch singing *Seeing Nellie Home*. And I'm invited over for lemonade. Come on back, Charley and Louisa. Keep looking till you find the third level! It's worth it, believe me!

The note was signed Sam.

At the stamp and coin store I go to, I found out that Sam bought $800 worth of old-style currency. That ought to set him up in a nice little hay, feed, and grain business; he always said that's what he really wished he could do, and he certainly can't go back to his old business. Not in Galesburg, Illinois, in 1894. His old business? Why, Sam was my psychiatrist.

The City of the Singing Flame

CLARK ASHTON SMITH

Clark Ashton Smith (1893-1961), poet, sculptor, and fantasist, was born in the gold-rush country of California, in the Sierra Nevada foothill town of Auburn, and spent most of his life there. In the 1920's and 1930's he was a member—perhaps the most gifted—of the circle of writers in contact with the great weird-tales author H. P. Lovecraft, and in those years Smith produced more than a hundred eerie, shimmering stories set in the lost continents of Atlantis and Hyperborea, on the yet unborn continent Zothique, and on worlds of other solar systems. His style—lush, evocative, extravagant in its use of uncommon words—must have seemed baffling and difficult to the readers of the pulp adventure magazines that published his work, and yet he won a devoted following and lived to see his stories collected in book form, books that now are cherished rarities.

One of Smith's most famous stories is "The City of the Singing Flame," which demonstrates the power of Smith's imagination without suffering from the fondness for strange adjectives that sometimes marred his work. Although regarded as a classic of fantasy, it has been out of print for many years. I hope it leads some readers to further discovery of the bizarre, haunting, altogether original tales of this neglected master of fantasy.

We had been friends for a decade or more, and I knew Giles Angarth as well as anyone could be said to know him. Yet the thing was no less a mystery to me than to others at the time; and it is still a mystery.

Sometimes I think that he and Felix Ebbonly had designed it all between them as a huge, insoluble hoax; that they are still alive somewhere, and are laughing at the world that has been so sorely baffled by their disappearance. And sometimes I make tentative plans to re-visit Crater Ridge and find, if I can, the boulders mentioned in Angarth's narrative as having a vague resemblance to broken-down columns.

In the meantime no one has uncovered any trace of the missing men or has heard even the faintest rumor concerning them. The whole affair, it would seem, is likely to remain a most singular and exasperating riddle.

Angarth, whose fame as a writer of fantastic fiction will probably outlive that of most other magazine contributors, had been spending the summer among the Sierras, and had been living alone until Ebbonly went to visit him. Ebbonly, whom I had never met, was well known for his imaginative paintings and drawings, and he had illustrated more than one of Angarth's novels. Neighboring campers became alarmed over the prolonged absence of the two men and searched the cabin for some possible clue. A package addressed to me was found lying on the table. I received it in due course of time, after reading many newspaper speculations regarding the double vanishment. The package contained a small, leather-bound notebook. Angarth had written on the flyleaf:

Dear Hastane:

You can publish this journal sometime, if you like. People will think it the last and wildest of all my fictions—unless they take it for one of your own. In either case, it will be just as well. Good-by.

Faithfully,
GILES ANGARTH

I am now publishing the journal, which will doubtless meet with the reception Angarth predicted. But I am not so certain myself, as to whether the tale is truth or fabrication. The only way to make sure will be to locate the two boulders; and anyone who has ever seen Crater Ridge, and has wandered over its miles of rock-strewn desolation, will realize the difficulties of such a task.

July 31st, 1930

I have never acquired the diary-keeping habit, mainly, I suppose, because of my uneventful mode of existence, in which there has seldom been anything to chronicle. But the thing which happened this morning is so extravagantly strange, so remote from mundane laws and parallels, that I feel impelled to write it down to the best of my understanding and ability. Also, I shall keep an account of the possible repetition and continuation of my experience. It will be perfectly safe to do this, for no one who ever reads the record will be likely to believe it.

I had gone for a walk on Crater Ridge, which lies a mile or less to the north of my cabin near Summit. Though differing markedly in its character from the usual landscapes roundabout, it is one of my favorite places. It is exceptionally bare and desolate, with little more in the way of vegetation than mountain sunflowers, wild currant bushes, and a few sturdy wind-warped pines and supple tamaracks.

Geologists deny it a volcanic origin. Yet its outcroppings of rough, nodular stone and enormous rubble-heaps have all the air of scoriaceous remains—at least, to my non-scientific eye. They look like the slag and refuse of Cyclopean furnaces, poured out in prehuman years to cool and harden into shapes of limitless grotesquery.

Among them are stones that suggest the fragments of primordial bas-reliefs, or small prehistoric idols and figurines. Others seem to have been graven with lost letters of an indecipherable script. Unexpectedly there is a little tarn lying on one end of the ridge, a tarn that has never been fathomed. The hill is an odd interlude among the granite sheets and crags, and the fir-clothed ravines and valleys of this region.

It was a clear, windless morning and I paused often to view the magnificent perspectives of varied scenery that were visible on every hand. I marveled at the titan battlements of Castle Peak, the rude masses of Donner Peak, with its dividing pass of hemlocks, the remote, luminous blue of the Nevada Mountains, and the soft green of willows in the valley at my feet. It was an aloof, silent world, and I heard no sound other than the dry, crackling noise of cicadas among the currant bushes.

I strolled on in a zigzag manner for quite some distance. Presently, coming to one of the rubble-fields with which the ridge is interstrewn, I began to search the ground closely, hoping to find a stone that was sufficiently quaint and grotesque in its form to be worth keeping as a curiosity. I had found several such in my previous wanderings.

Suddenly I came to a clear space amid the rubble, in which nothing grew—a space that was as round as an artificial ring. In the center were two isolated boulders, queerly alike in shape, and lying about five feet apart. I paused to examine them. Their substance, a dull, greenish-gray, seemed to be different from anything else in the neighborhood. I conceived at once the weird fancy that they might be pedestals of vanished columns, worn away by incalculable years till there remained only these sunken ends.

Certainly the perfect roundness and uniformity of the boulders were peculiar. And, though I possess a smattering of geology, I could not identify their smooth, soapy material.

My imagination was excited, and I began to indulge in some rather overheated fantasies. But the wildest of these was a homely commonplace in comparison with the thing that happened when I took a single step forward in the vacant space immediately between the two boulders. I shall try to describe it to the utmost of my verbal ability.

Nothing is more disconcerting than to miscalculate the degree of descent in taking a step. Imagine then what it was to find utter nothingness underfoot! I seemed to be going down into an empty gulf, and at the same time the landscape before me vanished in a swirl of broken images and everything went blind. There was a feeling of intense, Hyperborian cold. And indescribable sickness and vertigo possessed me, due, no doubt, to the profound disturbance of equilibrium.

Also—either from the speed of my descent or for some other reason—I was totally unable to draw breath.

My thoughts and feelings were unutterably confused. Half the time it seemed to me that I was falling upward rather than downward, or was sliding horizontally or at some oblique angle. At last I had the sensation of turning a complete somersault. Then I found myself standing erect on solid ground once more, without the least shock or jar of impact. The darkness cleared away from my vision, but I was still dizzy, and the optical images I received were altogether meaningless for some moments.

When I finally recovered enough to view my surroundings with a measure of perception, I experienced a mental confusion equivalent to that of a man who finds himself cast without warning on the shore of some foreign planet. There was the same sense of utter loss and alienation which would assuredly be felt in such a case—the same vertiginous, overwhelming bewilderment, the same ghastly sense of separation from all the familiar environmental details that give color and form and definition to our lives and even determine our very personalities.

I was standing in the midst of a landscape which bore no degree or manner of resemblance to Crater Ridge. A long, gradual slope, covered with violet grass and studded at intervals with stones of monolithic size and shape, ran undulantly away beneath me to a broad plain with sinuous, open meadows and high, stately forests of an unknown vegetation whose predominant hues were purple and yellow. The Plain seemed to end in a wall of impenetrable golden-brownish mist, that rose with phantom pinnacles to dissolve on a sky of luminescent amber in which there was no sun.

In the foreground of this amazing scene, not more than two or three miles away, there loomed a city whose massive towers and mountainous ramparts of red stone were such as the Anakim of undiscovered worlds might build. Wall on beetling wall, and spire on giant spire, it soared to confront the heavens, maintaining everywhere the severe and solemn lines of a rectangular architecture. It seemed to overwhelm and crush down the beholder with its stern and crag-like imminence.

As I viewed this city, I forgot my inital sense of bewildering loss and alienage, in an awe with which something of actual terror was mingled. At the same time, I felt an obscure but profound allurement, the cryptic emanation of some enslaving spell. But after I had gazed awhile, the cosmic strangeness and bafflement of my unthinkable position returned to me. Then, I felt only a wild desire to escape from the maddeningly oppressive bizarreness of this region and retain my own world. In an effort to fight down my agitation, I tried to figure out, if possible, what had really happened.

I had read a number of trans-dimensional stories. In fact, I had written one or two myself. I had often pondered the possibility of other worlds or material planes which may co-exist in the same space with ours, invisible and impalpable to human senses.

Of course, I realized at once that I had fallen into some such dimension. Doubtless, when I took that step forward between the boulders, I had been precipitated into some sort of flaw or fissure in space, to emerge at the bottom in this alien sphere—in a totally different kind of space. It sounded simple enough in a way, but not simple enough to make the modus operandi anything but a brain-racking mystery.

In a further effort to collect myself, I studied my immediate surroundings with close attention. This time, I was impressed by the arrangement of the monolithic stones I have spoken of, many of which were disposed at fairly regular intervals in two parallel lines running down the hill, as if to mark the course of some ancient road obliterated by the purple grass.

Turning to follow its ascent, I saw right behind me two columns, standing at precisely the same distance apart as the two odd boulders on Crater Ridge. They were made of the same greenish-gray stone! The pillars were perhaps nine feet high, and had been taller at one time, since the tops were splintered and broken away. Not far above them, the mounting slope vanished from view in a great bank of the same golden-brown mist that enveloped the remoter plain. But there were no more monoliths, and it seemed as if the road had ended with those pillars.

Inevitably I began to speculate as to the relationship between the columns in this new dimension and the boulders in my own world. Surely the resemblance could not be a matter of mere chance. If I stepped between the columns, could I return to the human sphere by a reversal of my precipitation therefrom? And if so, by what inconceivable beings from foreign time and space had the columns and boulders been established as the portals of a gateway between two worlds? Who could have used the gateway, and for what purpose?

My brain reeled before the infinite vistas of surmise that were opened by such questions.

However, what concerned me most was the problem of getting back to Crater Ridge. The weirdness of it all, the monstrous walls of the nearby town, the unnatural hues and forms of the outlandish scenery were too much for human nerves. I felt that I should go mad if forced to remain long in such a milieu. Also, there was no telling what hostile powers or entities I might encounter if I stayed.

The slope and plain were devoid of animal life, as far as I could see. But the great city was presumptive proof of human existence. Unlike the heroes of my own tales, who were wont to visit the fifth dimension or the worlds of Algol with perfect *sang froid*, I did not feel adventurous. Frankly, I shrank back with man's instinctive recoil before the unknown. With one fearful glance at the looming city and the wide plain with its lofty, gorgeous vegetation, I turned and stepped back between the columns.

There was the same instantaneous plunge into blind and freezing gulfs, the same indeterminate falling and twisting that had marked my descent into this new dimension. At the end I found myself standing, very dizzy and shaken, on the same spot from which I had taken my forward step between the greenish-gray boulders. Crater Ridge was swirling and reeling about me as if in the throes of earthquake. I had to sit down for a minute or two before I could recover my equilibrium.

I came back to the cabin like a man in a dream. The experience seemed, and still seems, incredible and unreal. Yet, it has overshadowed everything else, and has colored and dominated all my thoughts. Perhaps by writing it down I can shake it off a little.

It has unsettled me more than any previous experience in my whole life.

August 2nd

I have done a lot of thinking in the past few days and the more I ponder and puzzle, the more mysterious it all becomes. Granting the flaw in space, which must be an absolute vacuum, impervious to air, ether, light, and matter, how was it possible for me to fall into it? And having fallen in, how could I fall out—particularly into a sphere that has no certifiable relationship with ours?

But, after all, one process would be as easy as the other, in theory. The main objection is, how could one move in a vacuum, either up or down or backward or forward? The whole thing would baffle the comprehension of an Einstein; and I do not feel that I have approached the true solution.

Also, I have been fighting the temptation to go back, if only to convince myself that the thing really occurred. But, after all, why shouldn't I go back? An opportunity has been vouchsafed to me such as no man may ever have been given before. I am certain that the wonders I shall see and the secrets I shall learn are beyond imagining. My nervous trepidation is inexcusably childish under the circumstances.

I went back this morning, armed with a revolver. Somehow, without thinking that it might make a difference, I did not step in the very middle of the space between the boulders. Undoubtedly, as a result of this my descent was more prolonged and impetuous than before, and seemed to consist mainly of a series of spiral somersaults. It must have taken me minutes to recover from the ensuing vertigo. When I came to, I was lying on the violet grass.

This time, I went boldly down the slope. Keeping as much as I could in the shelter of that bizarre purple and yellow vegetation, I stole toward the looming city. All was very still. There was no breath of wind in those exotic trees, which appeared to imitate, in their lofty upright boles and horizontal foliage, the severe architectural lines of the Cyclopean buildings.

I had not gone very far when I came to a road in the forest, a road paved with stupendous blocks of stone at least twenty feet square. It ran toward the city. I thought for a while that it was wholly deserted, perhaps disused. I even dared walk upon it, till I heard a noise behind me and, turning, saw the approach of several singular entities. Terrified, I sprang back and hid myself in a thicket, from which I watched the passing of those creatures, wondering fearfully if they had seen me. Apparently my fears were groundless, for they did not even glance at my hiding place.

It is hard for me to describe or even visualize them now, for they were totally unlike anything that we are accustomed to think as human or animal. They must have been ten feet tall, and they were moving along with colossal strides that took them from sight in a few instants beyond a turn of the road. Their bodies were bright and shining, as if encased in some sort of armor. Their heads were equipped with high, curving appendages of opalescent hues which nodded above them like fantastic plumes, but which may have been antennae or other sense-organs of a novel type.

Trembling with excitement and wonder, I continued my progress through the richly colored undergrowth. As I went on, I perceived for the first time that there were no shadows anywhere. The light came from all portions of the sunless amber heaven, pervading everything with a soft, uniform luminosity.

All was motionless and silent, as I have said before. There was no evidence of bird, insect, or animal life in all this preternatural landscape. But when I had advanced to within a mile of the city (as well as I could judge the distance in a realm where the very proportions of objects were unfamiliar) I became aware of something which at first was recognizable as a vibration rather than a sound.

There was a queer thrilling in my nerves, the disquieting sense of some unknown force or emanation flowing through my body. This was perceptible for some time before I heard the music. But, having heard it, my auditory nerves identified it at once with the vibration.

It was faint and far-off, and seemed to emanate from the very heart of the titan city. The melody was piercingly sweet and resembled at times the singing of some voluptuous feminine voice. However, no human voice could have possessed the unearthly pitch, the shrill, perpetually sustained notes that somehow suggested the light of remote worlds and stars translated into sound.

Ordinarily I am not very sensitive to music. I have been reproached for not reacting more strongly to it. But I had not gone much farther when I realized the peculiar mental and emotional spell which the far-off sound was beginning to exert upon me. There was a sirenlike allurement which drew me on hypnotically, made me forget the strangeness and potential perils of my situation. I felt a slow, druglike intoxication of brain and senses. In some insidious manner, I know not how or why, the music conveyed the ideas of vast but attainable space and altitude, of superhuman freedom and exultation. It seemed to promise all the impossible splendors of which my imagination had vaguely dreamed.

The forest continued almost to the city walls. Peering from behind the final boscage, I saw their overwhelming battlements in the sky above me, and noted the flawless jointure of their prodigious blocks. I was near the great road, which entered an open gate that was large enough to admit the passage of behemoths.

There were no guards in sight, and several more of the tall gleaming entities came striding along and went in as I watched. From where I stood, I was unable to see inside the gate; for the wall was stupendously thick. The music poured from the mysterious entrance in an ever-strengthening flood and sought to draw me on with its weird seduction, eager for unimaginable things.

It was hard to resist, hard to rally my will power and turn back. I tried to concentrate on the thought of danger, but the thought was tenuously unreal. At last I tore myself away and retraced my footsteps, very slowly and lingeringly, till I was beyond reach of the music. Even then the spell persisted, like the effects of a drug, and all the way home I was tempted to return and follow those shining giants into the city.

August 5th

I have visited the new dimension once more. I thought I could resist that summoning music; and I even took some cotton-wadding along with which to stuff my ears if it should affect me too strongly. I began to hear the supernal melody at the same distance as before, and was drawn on in the same manner. But this time I entered the open gate.

I wonder if I can describe that city. I felt like a crawling ant upon its pavements, amid the measureless Babel of its buildings, of its streets and arcades. Everywhere there were columns, obelisks, and the perpendicular pylons of fane-like structures that would have dwarfed those of Thebes and Heliopolis.

And the people of the city! How is one to depict them or give them a name! I think that the gleaming entities I first saw are not the true inhabitants, but are only visitors—perhaps from another world of dimension, like myself. The real people are giants, too; but they move slowly, with solemn, hieratic paces.

Their bodies are swart and their limbs are those of caryatids—massive enough, it would seem, to uphold the roofs and lintels of their own buildings. I fear to describe them minutely. Human words would give the idea of something monstrous and uncouth. But these beings are not monstrous. They have merely developed in obedience to laws of another evolution than ours, the environmental forces and conditions of a different world.

Somehow, I was not afraid when I saw them. Perhaps the music had drugged me till I was beyond fear. There was a group of them just inside the gate, and they seemed to pay me no attention whatever as I passed them. The opaque, jetlike orbs of their huge eyes were impressive as the carven eyes of andro-sphinxes, and they uttered no sound from their heavy, straight, expressionless lips. Perhaps they lack the sense of hearing, for their strange, semi-rectangular heads were devoid of anything in the nature of external ears.

I followed the music, which was still remote and seemed to increase little in loudness. I was soon overtaken by several of those beings whom I had previously seen on the road outside the walls. They passed me quickly and disappeared in the labyrinth of buildings. After them there came other beings, of a less gigantic kind, and without the bright shards of armor worn by the first-comers. Then, overhead, two creatures with long, translucent, blood-colored wings, intricately veined and ribbed, came flying side by side and vanished behind the others. Their faces, featured with organs of unsurmisable use, were not those of animals. I felt sure that they were beings of a high order of development.

I saw hundreds of those slow-moving somber entities whom I have identified as the true inhabitants. None of them appeared to notice me. Doubtless they were accustomed to seeing far weirder and more unusual kinds of life than humanity. As I went on, I was overtaken by dozens of improbable-looking creatures, all going in the same direction as myself, as if drawn by the same siren melody.

Deeper and deeper I went into the wilderness of colossal architecture, led by that remote ethereal, opiate music. I soon noticed a sort of gradual ebb and flow in the sound, occupying an interval of ten minutes or more; but by imperceptible degrees it grew sweeter and nearer. I wondered how it could penetrate that manifold maze of stone and be heard outside the walls.

I must have walked for miles in the ceaseless gloom of those rectangular structures that hung above me, tier on tier, at an awful height in the amber zenith; then, at length, I came to the core and secret of it all. Preceded and followed by a number of those chimerical entities, I emerged on a great square in whose center was a temple-like building more immense than the others. The music poured, imperiously shrill and loud, from its many-columned entrance.

I felt the thrill of one who approaches the sanctum of some hierarchal mystery, when I entered the halls of that building. People who must have come from many different worlds or dimensions went with me and before me along the titanic colonnades whose pillars were graven with indecipherable runes and enigmatic bas-reliefs.

Also, the dark colossal inhabitants of the town were standing or roaming about, intent, like all the others, on their own affairs. None of these beings spoke, either to me or to one another, and though several eyed me casually, my presence was evidently taken for granted.

There are no words to convey the incomprehensible wonder of it all. And the music? I have utterly failed to describe that, also. It was as if some marvelous elixir had been turned into sound-waves—an elixir conferring the gift of superhuman life, and the high, magnificent dreams which are dreamed by immortals. It mounted in my brain like a supernal drunkenness as I approached the hidden source.

I do not know what obscure warning prompted me now to stuff my ears with cotton before I went any further. Though I could still hear it, still feel its peculiar, penetrant vibration, the sound became muted when I had done this and its influence was less powerful henceforward. There is little doubt that I owe my life to this simple and homely precaution.

The endless row of columns grew dim for awhile as the interior of a long basaltic cavern; and then, at some distance ahead, I perceived the glimmering of a soft light on the floor and pillars. The light soon became an overflooding radiance, as if some gigantic lamps were being lit in the temple's heart; and the vibrations of the hidden music pulsed more strongly in my nerves.

The hall ended in a chamber of immense, indefinite scope, whose walls and roof were doubtful with unremoving shadows. In the center, amid the pavement of mammoth blocks, there was a circular pit above which there seemed to float a fountain of flame that soared in one eerie, slowly lengthening jet. This flame was the sole illumination; and also it was the source of the wild, unearthly music. Even with my purposely deafened ears, I was wooed by the shrill and starry sweetness of its singing. I felt the voluptuous lure, the high, vertiginous exaltation.

I knew immediately that the place was a shrine, and the transdimension beings who accompanied me were visiting pilgrims. There were scores of them—perhaps hundreds; but all were dwarfed in the cosmic immensity of that chamber. They were gathered before the flame in various attitudes of worship. They bowed their heads or made mysterious gestures of adoration with unhuman hands and members. And the voices of several, deep as booming drums, or sharp as the stridulation of giant insects, were audible amind the singing of the fountain.

Spellbound, I went foward and joined them. Enthralled by the music and by the vision of the soaring flame, I paid as little heed to my outlandish compansions as they to me.

The fountain rose and rose, till its light flickered on the limbs and features of throned, colossal statues behind it—or heroes or gods or demons from the earlier cycles of alien time, staring in stone from a dusk of illimitable mystery. The fire was green and dazzling. It was pure as the central flame of a star.

It blinded me, and when I turned my eyes away, the air was filled with webs of intricate color, with swiftly changing arabesques whose numberless, unwonted hues and patterns were such as no mundane eye had ever beheld. I felt a stimulating warmth that filled my very marrow with intenser life.

The music mounted with the flame and I understood now its recurrent ebb and flow. As I looked and listened, a mad thought was born in my mind—the thought of how marvelous and ecstatical it would be to run forward and leap headlong into the singing fire. The music seemed to tell me that I should find in that moment of flaring dissolution all the delight and triumph, all the splendor and exaltation it had promised from afar. It besought me; it pleaded with tones of supernal melody. And despite the wadding in my ears, the seduction was well-nigh irresistible.

However, it had not robbed me of all sanity. With a sudden start of terror, like one who has been tempted to fling himself from a high precipice, I drew back. Then I saw that the same dreadful impulse was shared by some of my companions. The two entities with scarlet wings, whom I have previously mentioned, were standing a little apart from the rest of us. Now with a great fluttering, they rose and flew toward the flame like moths toward a candle. For a brief moment the light shone redly through their half-transparent wings, ere they disappeared in the leaping incandescence, which flared briefly and then burned as before.

Then, in rapid succession, a number of other beings, who represented the most divergent trends of biology, sprang forward and immolated themselves in the flame. There were creatures with translucent bodies, and some that shone with all the hues of the opal. There were winged colossi, and titans who strode as with seven-league boots. There was one being with useless, abortive wings who crawled rather than ran, to seek the same glorious doom as the rest. But among them there was none of the city's people. The city's inhabitants merely stood and looked on, impassive and statuelike as ever.

I saw that the fountain had now reached its greatest height and was beginning to decline. It sank steadily but slowly to half its former elevation. During this interval there were no more acts of self-sacrificing. Several of the beings beside me turned abruptly and went away, as if they had overcome the lethal spell.

One of the tall armored entities, as he left, addressed me in words that were like clarion notes, with unmistakable accents of warning. By a mighty effort of will in a turmoil of conflicting emotions, I followed him. At every step the madness and delirium of the music warred with my instincts of self-preservation. More than once, I started to go back. My homeward journey was as blurred and doubtful as the wanderings of a man in an opium-trance. The music sang behind me and told me of the rapture I had missed, of the flaming dissolution whose brief instant was better than aeons of mortal life.

August 9th

I have tried to go on with a new story, but have made no progress. Anything that I can imagine, or frame in language, seems flat and puerile beside the world of unsearchable mystery to which I have found admission. The temptation to return is more cogent than ever, the call of that remembered music is sweeter than the voice of a loved woman. And always I am tormented by the problem of it all, and tantalized by the little which I have perceived and understood. What forces are those whose existence and working I have merely apprehended? Who are the inhabitants of the city? And who are the beings that visit the enshrined flame? What rumor or legend has drawn them from outland realms to that place of blissful danger and destruction? And what is the fountain itself, and what the secret of its lure and its deadly singing? These problems admit of infinite surmise, but no conceivable solution.

I am planning to go back once more—but not alone. Someone must go with me this time, as a witness to the wonder and the peril. It is all too strange for credence—I must have human corroboration of what I have seen and felt and conjectured. Also, another might understand where I have failed to do more than apprehend.

Whom shall I take? It will be necessary to invite someone here from the outer world—someone of high intellectual and aesthetic capacity. Shall I ask Philip Hastane, my fellow fiction-writer? Hastane would be too busy, I fear. But there is the Californian artist, Felix Ebbonly, who has illustrated some of my fantastic novels.

Ebbonly would be the man to see and appreciate the new dimension, if he can come. With his bent for the bizarre and the unearthly, the spectacle of that plain and city, the Babelian buildings and arcades, and the temple of the flame, will simply enthrall him. I shall write immediately to his San Francisco address.

August 12th

Ebbonly is here—the mysterious hints in my letter regarding some novel pictorial subjects along his own line were too provocative for him to resist. Now I have explained fully and given him a detailed account of my adventures. I can see that he is a little incredulous, for which I hardly blame him. But he will not remain incredulous very long, for tomorrow we shall visit, together, the city of the singing flame.

August 13th

I must concentrate my disordered faculties. I must choose my words and write with exceeding care. This will be the last entry in my journal, and the last writing I shall ever do. When I have finished, I shall wrap the journal up and address it to Philip Hastane, who can make such disposition of it as he sees fit.

I took Ebbonly into the other dimension today. He was impressed, even as I had seen, by the two isolated boulders on Crater Ridge.

"They look like the guttered ends of columns established by prehuman gods," he remarked. "I begin to believe you now."

I told him to go first, and indicated the place where he should step. He obeyed without hesitation, and I had the singular experience of seeing a man melt into utter, instantaneous nothingness. One moment he was there—and the next, there was only bare ground and the far-off tamaracks whose view his body had obstructed. I followed and found him standing in speechless awe on the violet grass.

"This," he said at last, "is the sort of thing whose existence I have hitherto merely suspected, and have never even been able to hint at in my most imaginative drawings."

We spoke little as we followed the range of monolithic boulders toward the plain. Far in the distance, beyond those high and stately trees with their sumptuous foliage, the golden-brown vapors had parted, showing vistas of an immense horizon. Past the horizon were range on range of gleaming orbs and fiery, flying motes in the depths of the amber heaven. It was as if the veil of another universe than ours had been drawn back.

We crossed the plain, and came at length within earshot of the siren music. I warned Ebbonly to stuff his ears with cotton wadding. But he refused.

"I don't want to deaden any new sensation which I may experience," he observed.

We entered the city. My companion was a veritable rhapsody of artistic delight when he beheld the enormous buildings and the people. I could see, too, that the music had taken hold upon him. His look soon became fixed and dreamy as that of an opium-eater. At first he made many comments on the architecture and the various beings who passed us, and called my attention to details which I had not perceived heretofore.

However, as we drew nearer to the temple of the flame, his observational interest seemed to lag, and was replaced by more and more of an ecstatic inward absorption. His remarks became fewer and fewer. He did not even seem to hear my questions. It was evident that the sound had wholly bemused and bewitched him.

Even as on my former visit, there were many pilgrims going toward the shrine—and few that were coming away from it. Most of them belonged to the evolutionary types I had seen before. Among those that were new to me I recall one gorgeous creature with golden and cerulean wings like those of a giant lepidopteran and scintillating jewel-like eyes that must have been designed to mirror the glories of some Edenic world.

I, too, felt, as before, the captious thralldom and bewitchment, the insidious, gradual perversion of thought and instinct as if the music were working on my brain like a subtle alkaloid. Since I had taken my usual precaution, my subscription to the influence was less complete than that of Ebbonly. But nevertheless it was enough to make me forget a number of things— among them, the initial concern which I had felt when my companion had refused to employ the same mode of protection as myself. I no longer thought of his danger or my own, except as something very distant and immaterial.

The streets were like the prolonged and bewildering labyrinth of a nightmare. But the music led us forthrightly; and always there were other pilgrims. Like men in the grip of some powerful current we were drawn to our destination.

As we passed along the hall of gigantic columns and neared the abode of the fiery fountain, a sense of our peril quickened momentarily in my brain, and I sought to warn Ebbonly once more. But all my protests and remonstrances were futile. He was deaf as a machine, and wholly impervious to anything but the lethal music. His expression and his movements were those of a somnambulist. Even when I seized and shook him with such violence as I could muster, he remained oblivious of my presence.

The throng of worshippers was larger than upon my first visit. The jet of pure, incandescent flame was mounting steadily as we entered, and it sang with the pure ardor and ecstasy of a star alone in space. Again, with ineffable tones, it told me the rapture of a moth-like death in its lofty soaring, the exultation and triumph of a momentary union with its elemental essence.

The flame rose to its apex; and even for me, the mesmeric lure was well-nigh irresistible. Many of our companions succumbed. The first to immolate himself was the giant lepidopterous being. Four others, of diverse evolutionary types, followed in appallingly swift succession.

In my own partial subjection to the music, my own effort to resist that deadly enslavement, I had almost forgotten the very presence of Ebbonly. It was too late for me to even think of stopping him, when he ran forward in a series of leaps that were both solemn and frenzied, like the beginning of some sacerdotal dance, and hurled himself headlong into the flame. The fire enveloped him. It flared up for an instant with a more dazzling greenness. And that was all.

Slowly, as if from benumbed brain-centers, a horror crept upon my conscious mind, and helped to annul the perilous mesmerism. I turned, while many others were following Ebbonly's example, and fled from the shrine and from the city. But somehow the horror diminished as I went, and more and more I found myself envying my companion's fate, and wondering as to the sensations he had felt in that moment of fiery dissolution. . . .

Now, as I write this, I am wondering why I came back again to the human world. Words are futile to express what I have beheld and experienced, and the change that has come upon me beneath the play of incalculable forces in a world of which no other mortal is even cognizant.

Literature is nothing more than shadow. And life, with its drawn-out length of monotonous, reiterative days, is unreal and without meaning now in comparison with the splendid death which I might have had—the glorious doom which is still in store. I have no longer any will to fight the ever-insistent music which I hear in memory. And there seems to be no reason at all why I should fight it out. Tomorrow I shall return to the city.

The Sunken Land

FRITZ LEIBER

Of all of San Francisco's many literary figures, Fritz Leiber is probably the most conspicuous—not only because of his willingness to make public appearances, signing autographs or reading his own work on behalf of this charity or that, but also because of his giant stature and imposing presence. Surprisingly often, driving through the compact, foggy city by the bay, I see the towering form of Leiber striding through the mists, and honk and wave as I pass him by. He is eminent in more than height, though; few modern writers of fantasy and science fiction have achieved such popularity as he has, as his cluttered shelf of Hugo, Nebula, and miscellaneous other trophies attests. Perhaps his most widely beloved stories are those recounting the adventures of the giant barbarian Fafhrd and his wily companion, the Gray Mouser, in the world of Nehwon, which exists somewhere across the gulf of dimensions from our own. The chronicles of Fafhrd and the Gray Mouser fill at least five volumes by now, and Leiber, who has been writing them since 1939, still continues to return to Nehwon every few years. Here is one of the earliest of the series, a story of the Atlantis of Newhon, the lost land of Simorgya.

"I was born with luck as a twin!" roared Fafhrd jovially, leaping up so swiftly that the cranky sloop rocked a little in spite of its outriggers. "I catch a fish in the middle of the ocean. I rip up its belly. And look, little man, what I find!"

The Gray Mouser drew back from the fish-bloodied hand thrust almost into his face, wrinkled his nose with sneering fastidiousness, raised his left eyebrow and peered. The object did not seem very small even on Fafhrd's broad palm, and although slimed-over a little, was indubitably gold. It was both a ring and a key, the key part set at a right angle, so that it would lie along the finger when worn. There were carvings of some sort. Instinctively the Gray Mouser did not like the object. It somehow focused the vague uneasiness he had felt now for several days.

To begin with, he did not like the huge, salty Outer Sea, and only Fafhrd's bold enthusiasm and his own longing for the land of Lankhmar had impelled him to embark on this long, admittedly risky voyage across uncharted deeps. He did not like the fact that a school of fish was making the water boil at such a great distance from any land. Even the uniformly stormless weather and favorable winds disturbed him, seeming to indicate correspondingly great misfortunes held in store, like a growing thundercloud in quiet air. Too much good luck was always dangerous. And now this ring, acquired without effort by an astonishingly lucky chance.

They peered at it more closely, Fafhrd slowly turning it around. The carving on the ring part, as far as one could make out, represented a sea monster dragging down a ship. It was highly stylized, however, and there was little detail. One might be mistaken. What puzzled the Mouser most, since he had traveled to far places and knew much of the world, was that he did not recognize the style.

But in Fafhrd it roused strange memories. Recollections of certain legends told around flickering driftwood fires through the long Northern nights; tales of great seafarings and distant raids made in ancient days; firelight glimpses of certain bits of

THE SUNKEN LAND

loot taken by some unaccountably distant ancestor and considered too traditionally significant to barter or sell or even give away; ominous vague warnings used to frighten little boys who were inclined to swim or sail too far out. For a moment his green eyes clouded and his wind-burned face became serious, but only for a moment.

"A pretty enough thing, you'll agree," he said, laughing. "Whose door do you think it unlocks? Some king's mistress, I'd say. It's big enough for a king's finger." He tossed it up, caught it, and wiped it on the rough cloth of his tunic.

"I wouldn't wear it," said the Mouser. "It was probably eaten from a drowned man's hand and sucked poison from the sea ooze. Throw it back."

"And fish for a bigger one?" asked Fafhrd, grinning. "No, I'm content with this." He thrust it down on the middle finger of his left hand, doubled up his fist, and surveyed it critically. "Good for bashing people with, too," he remarked.

Then, seeing a big fish flash out of the water and almost flop into the cockpit, he snatched up his bow, fitted to the string a featherless arrow whose head was barbed and heavily weighted, and stared down over the side, one foot extended along the outrigger. A light, waxed line was attached to the arrow.

The Mouser watched him, not without envy. Fafhrd, big rangy man that he was, seemed to acquire an altogether new litheness and sureness of movement whenever they were on shipboard. He became as nimble as the Mouser was on shore. The Mouser was no landlubber and could swim as well as Fafhrd, but he always felt a trifle uneasy when there was only water in sight, day in and day out, just as Fafhrd felt uneasy in cities, though relishing taverns and street fights. On shipboard the Mouser became cautious and apprehensive; he made a point of watching for slow leaks, creeping fires, tainted food and rotten cordage. He disapproved of Fafhrd's constant trying out of new rigs and waiting until the last moment before reefing sail. It irked him a little that he couldn't quite call it foolhardy.

Fafhrd continued to scan intently the swelling, sliding

waters. His long, copper-red hair was shoved back over his ears and knotted securely. He was clothed in rough brownish tunic and trousers. Light leather slippers, easily kicked off, were on his feet. Belt, longsword, and other weapons were, of course, wrapped away in oiled cloth against corrosion and rust. And there were no jewels or ornaments, save for the ring.

The Mouser's gaze shifted past him to where clouds were piling up a little on the horizon off the bow to starboard. He wondered, almost with relief, whether this mightn't be the dirty weather due them. He pulled his thin gray tunic closer at his throat and shifted the tiller a little. The sun, near setting, projected his crouching shadow against the brownish sail.

Fafhrd's bow twanged and the arrow plummeted. Line hissed from the reel he held in his arrow hand. He checked it with his thumb. It slackened a trifle, then jerked off toward the stern. Fafhrd's foot slid along the outrigger until it stopped against the pontoon, a good three arms'-lengths from the side. He let the other foot slide after it and lay there effortlessly braced, sea drenching his legs, playing the fish carefully, laughing and grunting satisfiedly.

"And what was your luck this time?" the Mouser asked afterward, as Fafhrd served them smoking-hot, white tender flesh boiled over the firebox in the snug cabin forward. "Did you get a bracelet and necklace to match the ring?"

Fafhrd grinned with his mouth full and did not answer, as if there were nothing in the world to do but eat. But when they stretched themselves out later in the starry, cloud-broken darkness alive with a racing wind from starboard that drove their craft along at an increasing speed, he began to talk.

"I think they called the land Simorgya. It sank under the sea ages ago. Yet even then my people had gone raiding against it, though it was a long sail out and a weary beat homeward. My memory is uncertain. I only heard scraps of talk about it when I was a little child. But I did see a few trinkets carved somewhat like this ring; just a very few. The legends, I think, told that the men of far Simorgya were mighty magicians, claiming power over wind and waves and all the creatures below. Yet the sea gulped them down for all that. Now they're there." He rotated his hand until his thumb pointed at the bottom of the boat. "My people, the legends say, went raiding against them one summer, and none of the boats returned, save one, which came back after hope had been lost, its men almost dead from thirst. They told of sailing on and on, and never reaching Simorgya, never sighting its rocky coast and squat, many-windowed towers. Only the empty sea. More raiders went out the next summer and the next, yet none ever found Simorgya."

"But in that case," questioned the Mouser sharply, "may we not even now be sailing over that sunken land? May not that very fish you caught have swum in and out the windows of those towers?"

"Who can say?" answered Fafhrd, a little dreamily. "The ocean's big. If we're where we think we are—that is, almost home—it might be the case. Or not. I do not know if there ever really was a Simorgya. The legend-makers are great liars. In any case, that fish could hardly have been so ancient as to have eaten the flesh of a man of Simorgya."

"Nevertheless," said the Mouser in a small, flat voice, "I'd throw the ring away."

Fafhrd chuckled. His imagination was stirred, so that he saw the fabled land of Simorgya, not lightless and covered with great drifts of sea ooze, but as it once might have been, alive with ancient industry and commerce, strong with alien wizardry. Then the picture changed and he saw a long, twenty-oared galley, such as his people made, driving ahead into a stormy sea. There was the glint of gold and steel about the captain on the poop, and the muscles of the steersman cracked as he strained at the steering oar. The faces of the warrior-rowers were exultantly eager, dominated by the urge to rape the unknown. The whole ship was like a thirsty spearhead. He marveled at the vividness of the picture. Old longings vibrated faintly in his flesh. He felt the ring, ran his finger over the carving of the ship and monster, and again chuckled.

The Mouser fetched a stubby, heavy-wicked candle from the cabin and fixed it in a small horn lantern that was proof against the wind. Hanging at the stern it pushed back the darkness a little, not much. Until midnight it was the Mouser's watch. After a while Fafhrd slumbered.

He awoke with the feeling that the weather had changed and quick work was wanted. The Mouser was calling him. The sloop had heeled over so that the starboard pontoon rode the crests of the waves. There was chilly spray in the wind. The lantern swung wildly. Only astern were stars visible. The Mouser brought the sloop into the wind, and Fafhrd took a triple reef in the sail, while waves hammered the bow, an occasional light crest breaking over.

When they were on their course again, he did not immediately join the Mouser, but stood wondering, for almost the first time, how the sloop would stand heavy seas. It was not the sort of boat he would have built in his Northern homeland, but it was the best that could be gotten under the circumstances. He had caulked and tarred it meticulously, replaced any wood that looked too weak, substituted a triangular sail for the square one, and increased the height of the bow a trifle. To offset a tendency to capsize, he had added outriggers a little astern of the mast, getting the strongest, truest wood for the long crosspieces, carefully steaming them into the proper shape. It was a good job, he knew, but that didn't change the fact that the boat had a clumsy skeleton and many hidden weaknesses. He sniffed the raw, salt air and peered to windward through narrowed eyes, trying to gauge the weather. The Mouser was saying something, he realized, and he turned his head to listen.

"Throw the ring away before she blows a hurricane!"

He smiled and made a wide gesture that meant No. Then he turned back to gaze at the wild glimmering chaos of darkness and waves to windward. Thoughts of the boat and the weather dropped away, and he was content to drink in the awesome, age-old scene, swaying to keep balance, feeling each movement of the boat and at the same time sensing, almost as if it

THE SUNKEN LAND

were something akin to himself, the godless force of the elements.

It was then the thing happened that took away his power to react and held him, as it were, in a spell. Out of the surging wall of darkness emerged the dragon-headed prow of a galley. He saw the black wood of the sides, the light wood of the ears, the glint of wet metal. It was so like the ship of his imaginings that he was struck dumb with wonder as to whether he had had a foreglimpse of it by second sight, or whether he had actually summoned it across the deeps by his thoughts. It loomed higher, higher, higher.

The Mouser cried out and pushed over the tiller, his body arched with the mighty effort. Almost too late the sloop came out of the path of the dragon-headed prow. And still Fafhrd stared as at an apparition. He did not hear Mouser's warning shout as the sloop's sail filled from the other side and slammed across with a rush. The boom caught him in the back of the knees and hurled him outward, but not into the sea, for his feet found the narrow pontoon and he balanced there precariously. In that instant an oar of the galley swung down at him and he toppled sideways, instinctively grasping the blade as he fell. The sea drenched him and wrenched at him, but he clung tightly and began to pull himself up the oar, hand over hand.

His legs were numb from the blows; he feared he would be unable to swim. And he was still bewitched by what he saw. For the moment he forgot the Mouser and the sloop entirely. He shook off the greedy waves, reached the side of the galley, caught hold of the oar-hole. Then he looked back and saw, in a kind of stupid surprise, the disappearing stern of the sloop and the Mouser's gray-capped face, revealed by a close swing of the lantern, staring at him in blank helplessness.

What happened next ended whatever spell had held him. A hand that carried steel struck. He twisted to one side and caught the wrist, then grasped the side of the galley, got his foot in the oar-hole, on top of the oar, and heaved. The man dropped the knife too late, clawed at the side, failed to get a secure hold, and was dragged overboard, spitting and snapping his jaws in futile panic. Fafhrd, instinctively taking the offensive, sprang down onto the oarbench, which was the last of ten and half under the poop deck. His questioning eyes spied a rack of swords and he whirled one out, menacing the two shadowy figures hastening toward him, one from the forward oarbenches, one from the poop. They attacked with a rush, but silently, which was strange. The spray-wet weapons sparkled as they clashed.

Fafhrd fought warily, on guard for a blow from above, timing his lunges to the roll of the galley. He dodged a swashing blow and parried an unexpected back-handed slash from the same weapon. Stale, sour wine fumes puffed into his face. Someone dragged out an oar and thrust it like a huge lance; it came between Fafhrd and the two swordsmen, crashing heavily into the sword rack. Fafhrd glimpsed a rat-like, beady-eyed, toothy face peering up at him from the deeper darkness under the poop. One of the swordsmen lunged wildly, slipped and fell. The other gave ground, then gathered himself for a rush. But he paused with his sword in midair, looking over Fafhrd's head as if at a new adversary. The crest of a great wave struck him in the chest, obscuring him.

Fafhrd felt the weight of the water on his shoulders and clutched at the poop for support. The deck was at a perilous tilt. Water gushed up through the opposite oarholes. In the confusion, he realized, the galley had gotten into the troughs, and was beginning to take the seas broadside. She wasn't built to stand that. He vaulted up out of another breaking wave onto the poop and added his strength to that of the lone struggling steersman. Together they strained at the great oar, which seemed to be set in stone instead of water. Inch by inch, they fought their way across the narrow deck. None the less, the galley seemed doomed.

Then something—a momentary lessening of the wind and waves or perhaps a lucky pull by a forward oarsman—decided the issue. As slowly and laboriously as a waterlogged hulk the galley lifted and began to edge back into the proper course.

Fafhrd and the steersman strained prodigiously to hold each foot gained. Only when the galley was riding safe before the wind did they look up. Fafhrd saw two swords leveled steadily at his chest. He calculated his chances and did not move.

It was not easy to believe that fire had been preserved through that tremendous wetting, but one of the swordsmen nevertheless carried a sputtering tarry torch. By its light Fafhrd saw that they were Northerners akin to himself. Big raw-boned fellows, so blond, they seemed almost to lack eyebrows. They wore metal-studded war gear and close-fitting bronze helmets. Their expressions were frozen halfway between a glare and a grin. Again he smelled stale wine. His glance strayed forward. Three oarsmen were bailing with bucket and hand crane.

Somebody was striding toward the poop—the leader, if one could guess from the gold and jewels and an air of assurance. He sprang up the short ladder, his limbs supple as a cat's. He seemed younger than the rest and his features were almost delicate. Fine, silky blond hair was plastered wetly against his cheeks. But there was feline rapacity in his tight, smiling lips, and there was craziness in his jewel-blue eyes. Fafhrd hardened his own face against their inspection. One question kept nagging him. Why, even at the height of the confusion, had there been no cries, no shouts, no bellowed orders? Since he had come aboard, there had not been a word uttered.

The young leader seemed to come to a conclusion about Fafhrd, for his thin smile widened a trifle and he motioned toward the oar deck. Then Fafhrd broke silence and said in a voice that sounded unnatural and hoarse, "What do you intend? Weigh well the fact that I saved your ship."

He tensed himself, noting with some satisfaction that the steersman stayed close beside him, as if their shared task had forged a bond between them. The smile left the leader's face. He laid his fingers to his lips and then impatiently repeated his first gesture. This time Fafhrd understood. He was to replace the oarsman he had pulled overboard. He could not but admit there was a certain ironic justice to the idea. It was borne in on him that swift death would be his lot if he renewed the fight at such a disadvantage; slow death, if he leaped overboard in the mad hope of finding the sloop in the howling, heaving darkness. The arms holding the swords became taut. He curtly nodded his head in submission. At least they were his own people.

With his first feel of the heavy, rebellious water against the blade of his oar, a new feeling took hold of Fafhrd—a feeling with which he was not unfamiliar. He seemed to become part of the ship, to share its purposes, whatever they might be. It was the age-old spirit of the oarbench. When his muscles had warmed to the task and his nerves became accustomed to the rhythm, he found himself stealing glances at the men around him, as if he had known them before; trying to penetrate and share the eager, set look on their faces.

Something huddled in many folds of ragged cloth shuffled out from the little cabin far back under the poop and held a leather flask to the lips of the opposite oarsman. The creature looked absurdly squat among such tall men. When it turned Fafhrd recognized the beady eyes he had glimpsed before and, as it came nearer, distinguished under the heavy cowl the wrinkled, subtle, ocher face of an aged Mingol.

"So you're the new one," the Mingol croaked jeeringly. "I liked your swordplay. Drink deep now, for Lavas Laerk may decide to sacrifice you to the sea gods before morning. But, mind you, don't dribble any."

Fafhrd sucked greedily, then almost coughed and spat when a rush of strong wine seared his throat. After a while the Mingol jerked the flask away.

"Now you know what Lavas Laerk feeds his oarsmen. There are few crews in this world or the next that row on wine." He chuckled, then said, "But you're wondering why I talk aloud. Well, young Lavas Laerk may put a vow of silence on all his men, but he may not do the same to me, who is only a slave. For I tend the fire—how carefully you must know—and serve out the wine and cook the meat, and recite incantations for the good of the ship. There are certain things that neither Lavas Laerk nor any other man, nor any other demon, may demand of me."

"But what does Lavas Laerk—"

The Mingol's leathery palm clapped over Fafhrd's mouth and shut off the whispered question.

"Sh! Do you care so little for life? Remember, you are Lavas Laerk's henchman. But I will tell you what you would know." He sat down on the wet bench beside Fafhrd, looking like a bundle of rags someone had dropped there. "Lavas Laerk has sworn to raid far Simorgya, and he has put a vow of silence upon himself and his men until they sight the coast. Sh! Sh! I know they say Simorgya is under the waves, or that there never was such a place. But Lavas Laerk swore a great oath before his mother, whom he hates worse than he hates his friends, and he killed a man who thought to question his decision. So it's Simorgya we seek, if only to steal pearls from the oysters and ravish the fishes. Lean down and row more easily for a space, and I will tell you a secret that's no secret and make a prophecy that's no prophecy." He crowded closer. "Lavas Laerk hates all men who are sober, for he believes—and rightly—that only drunken men are even a little like himself. Tonight the crew will row well, though it's a day since they've had meat. Tonight the wine will make them see at least the glow of the visions that Lavas Laerk sees. But next morning there will be aching backs and sick guts and pain-hammered skulls. And then there will be mutiny and not even Lavas Laerk's madness will save him."

Fafhrd wondered by the Mingol shuddered, coughed weakly and made a gargling sound. He reached over and a warm fluid drenched his naked hand. Then Lavas Laerk pulled his dirk from the Mingol's neck and the Mingol rolled forward off the bench.

No word was spoken, but knowledge that some abominable deed had been committed passed from oarsman to oarsman through the stormy darkness until it reached the bench in the bow. Then gradually there began a kind of pent-up commotion, which increased markedly as there slowly percolated forward an awareness of the specially heinous nature of the deed—the murder of the slave who tended the fire and whose magical powers, though often scoffed at, were entwined with the destiny of the ship itself. Still no completely intelligible words, but low grunts and snarls and mutterings, the scrape of oars being drawn in and rested, a growing murmur in which consternation and fear and danger were mixed, and which washed back and forth between bow and poop like a wave in a tub. Half caught up by it, Fafhrd readied himself for a spring, though whether at the apprehensive motionless figure of Lavas Laerk or back toward the comparative safety of the poop cabin, he could not say. Certainly Lavas Laerk was doomed; or rather he would have been doomed, had not the steersman screamed from the poop in a great shaky voice, "Land ho! Simorgya! Simorgya!"

That wild cry, like a clawed skeletal hand, seized upon the agitation of the crew and wrenched it to an almost unbearable climax. A shuddering inhalation of breath swept the ship. Then came shouts of wonder, cries of fear, curses that were half prayers. Two oarsmen started to fight together for no other reason than that the sudden, painful upgush of feeling demanded action of some sort, any sort. Another pushed wildly at his oar, screeching at the rest to follow his example and reverse the galley's course and so escape. Fafhrd vaulted up on his bench and stared ahead.

It loomed up vast as a mountain and perilously close. A great black blot vaguely outlined by the lesser darkness of the night, partly obscured by trailings of mist and scud, yet showing in various places and at varying distances squares of dim light which by their regular arrangement could be nothing but windows. And with each pounding heartbeat the roar of surf and the thunder of breaking waves grew louder.

All at once it was upon him. Fafhrd saw a great overhanging crag slide by, so close it snapped the last oar on the opposite side. As the galley lifted on a wave he looked awestruck into three windows in the crag—if it was a crag and not a

THE SUNKEN LAND

half-submerged tower—but saw nothing save a ghostly yellow luminescence. Then he heard Lavas Laerk bellowing commands in a harsh, high-pitched voice. A few of the men worked frantically at the oars, but it was too late for that, although the galley seemed to have gotten behind some protecting wall of rock into slightly calmer water. A terrible rasping noise went the length of the keel. Timbers groaned and cracked. A last wave lifted them and a great grinding crash sent men reeling and tumbling. Then the galley stopped moving altogether and the only sound was the roar of the surf, until Lavas Laerk cried exultantly, "Serve out weapons and wine! Make ready for a raid!"

These words seemed incredible in this more than dangerous situation, with the galley broken beyond repair, gutted by the rocks. Yet the men rallied and seemed even to catch something of the wild eagerness of their master, who had proved to them that the world was no more sane than he.

Fafhrd watched them fetch torch after torch from the poop cabin, until the whole stern of the wreck smoked and flared. He watched them snatch and suck at the wineskins and heft the swords and dirks given out, comparing them and cleaving at the air to get the feel. Then some of them grabbed hold of him and hustled him to the sword rack, saying, "Here, Red Hair, you must have a weapon, too." Fafhrd went along unresisting, yet he felt that something would prevent them from arming one who so late had been their enemy. And he was right in this, for Lavas Laerk stopped the lieutenant who was about to hand Fafhrd a sword, and stared with growing intentness at Fafhrd's left hand.

Puzzled, Fafhrd raised it, and Lavas Laerk cried, "Seize him!" and at the same instant jerked something from Fafhrd's middle finger. Then Fafhrd remembered. It was the ring.

"There can be no doubt about the workmanship," said Lavas Laerk, peering cunningly at Fafhrd, his bright blue eyes giving the impression of being out of focus or slightly crossed. "This man is a Simorgyan spy, or perhaps a Simorgyan demon who has taken the form of a Northerner to allay our suspicions. He climbed out of the sea in the teeth of a roaring storm, did he not? What man among you saw any boat?"

"I saw a boat," ventured the steersman hurriedly. "A queer sloop with triangular sail—" But Lavas Laerk shut him up with a sidewise glance.

Fafhrd felt the point of the dirk at his back and checked his tightening muscles.

"Shall we kill him?" The question came from close behind Fafhrd's ear.

Lavas Laerk smiled crookedly up at the darkness and paused, as if listening to the advise of some invisible storm wraith. Then he shook his head. "Let him live for the present. He can show us where the loot is hid. Guard him with naked swords."

Whereupon they all left the galley, clambering down ropes hung from the prow onto rocks which the surf alternately covered and uncovered. One or two laughed and jumped. A dropped torch hissed out in the brine. There was much shouting. Someone began to sing in a drunken voice that had an edge like a rusty knife. Then Lavas Laerk got them into a sort of order and they marched away, half of them carrying torches, a few still hugging wineskins, sliding and slipping, cursing the sharp rocks and barnacles which cut them when they fell, hurling exaggerated threats at the darkness ahead, where strange windows glowed. Behind them the long galley lay like a dead beetle, the oars sprawled out all askew from the ports.

They had marched for some little distance, and the sound of the breakers was less thunderous, when their torchlight helped reveal a portal in the great wall of black rock that might or might not have been a castle rather than a caverned cliff. The portal was square and high as an oar. Three worn steps drifted with wet sand led up to it. Dimly they could discern on the pillars, and on the heavy lintel overhead, carvings partly obliterated by slime and incrustations of some sort, but unmistakably Simorgyan in their obscure symbolism.

The crew, staring silently now, drew closer together. The ragged procession became a tight knot. Then Lavas Laerk called mockingly, "Where are your guards, Simorgya? Where are your fighting men?" and walked straight up the stone steps. After a moment of uncertainty, the knot broke and the men followed him.

On the massive threshold Fafhrd involuntarily halted, dumbstruck by realization of the source of the faint yellow light he had earlier noticed on the high windows. For the source was everywhere: ceiling, walls, and slimy floor all glowed with a wavering phosphorescence. Even the carvings glimmered. Mixed awe and repugnance gripped him. But the men pressed around and against him, and carried him forward. Wine and leadership had dulled their sensibilities, and as they strode down the long corridor they seemed little aware of the abysmal scene.

At first some held their weapons ready to meet a possible foray or ambush, but soon they lowered them negligently, and even sucked at the wineskins and jested. A hulking oarsman, whose blond beard was patched with yellow scud from the surf, struck up a chantey and others joined in, until the dank walls roared. Deeper and deeper they penetrated into the cave or castle, along the wide, winding, ooze-carpeted corridor.

Fafhrd was carried along by a current. When he moved too slowly, the others jostled him and he quickened his pace, but it was all involuntary. Only his eyes responded to his will, turning from side to side, drinking in details with fearful curiosity: the endless series of vague carvings, wherein sea monsters and unwholesome manlike figures and vaguely anthropomorphic giant skates or rays seemed to come alive and stir as the phosphorescence fluctuated; a group of highest windows or openings of some sort, from which dark slippery weeds trailed down; the pools of water here and there; the still-alive, gasping fish, which the others trod or kicked aside; the clumps of bearded shells clinging to the corners; the impression of things scuttling out of the way ahead. Louder and louder the thought drummed in his skull: surely the others must realize where they were. Surely they must know the phosphorescence was that of the sea. Surely they must know that this was the retreat of the more secret creatures of the deep. Surely, surely they must know that Simorgya had indeed sunk under the sea and only risen up yesterday—or yester-hour.

But on they marched after Lavas Laerk, and still sang and shouted and swilled wine in quick gulps, throwing back their heads and lifting up the sacks as they strode. And Fafhrd could not speak. His shoulder muscles were contracted as if the weight of the sea were already pressing them down. His mind was engulfed and oppressed by the ominous presence of sunken Simorgya. Memories of the legends. Thoughts of the black centuries during which sea life had slowly crept and wiggled and swum through the mazes of rooms and corridors until it had a lair in every crack and cranny and Simorgya was one with the mysteries of the ocean. In a deep grotto that opened on the corridor he made out a thick table of stone, with a great stone chair behind it; and though he could not be sure, he thought he distinguished an octopus shape slouched there in a travesty of a human occupant, tentacles coiling the chair, unblinking eyes staring glisteningly.

Gradually the flare of the smoky torches paled, as the phosphorescence grew stronger. And when the men broke off singing, the sound of the surf was no longer audible.

Then Lavas Laerk, from around a sharp turn in the corridor, uttered a triumphant cry. The others hastened after, stumbling, lurching, calling out eagerly.

"Oh, Simorgya!" cried Lavas Laerk. "We have found your treasure house!"

The room in which the corridor ended was square and considerably lower-ceilinged than the corridor. Standing here and there were a number of black, soggy-looking, heavily bound chests. The stuff underfoot was muckier. There were more pools of water. The phosphorescence was stronger.

A blond-bearded oarsman leaped ahead as the others hesitated. He wrenched at the cover of the nearest chest. A corner came away in his hands, the wood soft as cheese, the seeming metal a black, smeary ooze. He grasped at it again and pulled off most of the top, revealing a layer of dully-gleaming gold and slime-misted gems. Over that jeweled surface a crab-like creature scuttled, escaping through a hole in the back.

With a great, greedy shout, the others rushed at the chests, jerking, gouging, even smiting with their swords at the spongy wood. Two, fighting as to which should break open a chest, fell against it and it went to pieces under them, leaving them struggling in jewels and muck.

All this while Lavas Laerk stood on the same spot from which he had uttered his first taunting cry. To Fafhrd, who stood forgotten beside him, it seemed that Lavas Laerk was distraught that his quest should come to any end, that Lavas Laerk was desperately searching for something further, something more than jewels and gold to sate his mad willfulness. Then he noted that Lavas Laerk was looking at something intently—a square, slime-filmed, but apparently golden door across the room from the mouth of the corridor; upon it was the carving of some strange, undulant blanket-like sea monster. He heard Lavas Laerk laugh throatily and watched him stride unswervingly toward the door. He saw that Lavas Laerk had something in his hand. With a shock of surprise he recognized it as the ring Lavas Laerk had taken from him. He saw Lavas Laerk shove at the door without budging it. He saw Lavas Laerk fumble with the ring and fit the key part into the golden door and turn it. He saw the door give a little to Lavas Laerk's next push.

Then he realized—and the realization came with an impact like a rushing wall of water—that nothing had happened accidentally, that everything from the moment his arrow struck the fish had been intended by someone or something— something that wanted a door unlocked—and he turned and fled down the corridor as if a tidal wave were sucking at his heels.

The corridor, without torchlight, was pale and shifty as a nightmare. The phosphorescence seemed to crawl as if alive, revealing previously unspied creatures in every niche. Fafhrd stumbled, sprawled at full length, raced on. His fastest bursts of speed seemed slow, as in a bad dream. He tried to look only ahead, but still glimpsed from the corners of his eyes every detail he had seen before: the trailing weeds, the monstrous carvings, the bearded shells, the somberly staring octopus eyes. He noted without surprise that his feet and body glowed wherever the slime had splashed or smeared. He saw a small square of darkness in the omnipresent phosphorescence and sprinted toward it. It grew in size. It was the cavern's portal. He plunged across the threshold into the night. He heard a voice calling his name.

It was the Gray Mouser's voice. It came from the opposite direction to the wrecked galley. He ran toward it across treacherous ledges. Starlight, now come back, showed a black gulf before his feet. He leaped, landed with a shaking impact on another rock surface, dashed forward without falling. He saw the top of a mast above an edge of darkness and almost bowled over the small figure that was staring raptly in the direction from which he had just fled. The Mouser seized him by the shoulder, dragged him to the edge, pulled him over. They clove the water together and swam out to the sloop anchored in the rock-sheltered lee. The Mouser started to heave at the anchor but Fafhrd slashed the line with a knife snatched from the Mouser's belt and jerked up the sail in swift, swishing rushes.

Slowly the sloop began to move. Gradually the ripples became wavelets, the wavelets became smacking waves. Then they slipped past a black, foam-edged sword of rock and were in the open sea. Still Fafhrd did not speak, but crowded on all canvas and did all else possible to coax speed from the storm-battered sloop. Resigned to mystification, the Mouser helped him.

They had not been long underway when the blow fell. The Mouser, looking sternward, gave a hoarse incredulous cry. The wave swiftly overtaking them was higher than the mast. And something was sucking the sloop back. The Mouser raised his arms shieldingly. Then the sloop began to climb; up, up, up until it reached the top, overbalanced, and plummeted down on the opposite side. The first wave was followed by a second and a third, and a fourth, each almost as high. A larger boat would surely have been swamped. Finally the waves gave way to a choppy, foaming, unpredictable chaos, in which every ounce of effort and a thousand quick decisions were needed to keep the sloop afloat.

When the pale foredawn came, they were back on the homeward course again, a small improvised sail taking the place of the one ripped in the aftermath of the storm, enough water bailed from the hold to make the sloop seaworthy. Fafhrd, dazedly watching for the sunrise, felt weak as a woman. He only half heard the Mouser tell, in snatches, of how he had lost the galley in the storm, but followed what he guessed to be its general course until the storm cleared, and had sighted the strange island and landed there, mistakenly believing it to be the galley's home port.

The Mouser then brought thin, bitter wine and salt fish, but Fafhrd pushed them away and said, "One thing I must know. I never looked back. You were staring earnestly at something behind me. What was it?"

The Mouser shrugged his shoulders. "I don't know. The distance was too great and the light was queer. What I thought I saw was rather foolish. I'd have given a good deal to have been closer." He frowned, shrugged his shoulders again. "Well, what I thought I saw was this: a crowd of men wearing big black cloaks—they looked like Northerners—came rushing out of an opening of some sort. There was something odd about them: the light by which I saw them didn't seem to have any source. Then they waved the big black cloaks around as if they were fighting with them or doing some sort of dance . . . I told you it was very foolish . . . and then they got down on their hands and knees and covered themselves up with the cloaks and crawled back into the place from which they had come. Now tell me I'm a liar."

Fafhrd shook his head. "Only those weren't cloaks," he said.

The Mouser began to sense that there was much more to it than he had even guessed. "What were they, then?" he asked.

"I don't know," said Fafhrd.

"But then what was the place, I mean the island that almost sucked us down when it sank?"

"Simorgya," said Fafhrd and lifted his head and began to grin in a cruel, chilly, wild-eyed way that took the Mouser aback. "Simorgya," repeated Fafhrd, and pulled himself to the side of the boat and glared down at the rushing water. "Simorgya. And now it's sunk again. And may it soak there forever and rot in its own corruption, till all's muck!" He trembled spasmodically with the passion of his curse, then sank back. Along the rim of the east a ruddy smudge began to show.

The Balloon Tree

EDWARD PAGE MITCHELL

Edward Page Mitchell (1852-1927) is one of the most obscure of the nineteenth-century pioneers of science fiction. He wrote dozens of stories for the famous New York newspaper The Sun, *and in them he dealt with time machines, invisibility, thinking machines, suspended animation, and many other themes later to become familiar material for science fiction. But because Mitchell's stories were published anonymously and because most of them appeared in so ephemeral a medium as a daily newspaper, his work was almost entirely forgotten until rediscovered in 1973 by science fiction's indefatigable historian, Sam Moskowitz. Here is one of Mitchell's most delectable stories, a tale of a mysterious island, a strange cult, and one of the most remarkable members of the plant kingdom ever to spring from a writer's imagination.*

I

The colonel said:

We rode for several hours straight from the shore toward the heart of the island. The sun was low in the western sky when we left the ship. Neither on the water nor on the land had we felt a breath of air stirring. The glare was upon everything. Over the low range of hills miles away in the interior hung a few copper-colored clouds. "Wind," said Briery. Kilooa shook his head.

Vegetation of all kinds showed the effects of the long continued drought. The eye wandered without relief from the sickly russet of the undergrowth, so dry in places that leaves and stems crackled under the horses' feet, to the yellowish-brown of the thirsty trees that skirted the bridle path. No growing thing was green except the bell-top cactus, fit to flourish in the crater of a living volcano.

Kilooa leaned over in the saddle and tore from one of these plants its top, as big as a California pear and bloated with juice. He crushed the bell in his fist, and, turning, flung into our hot faces a few grateful drops of water.

Then the guide began to talk rapidly in his language of vowels and liquids. Briery translated for my benefit.

The god Lalala loved a woman of the island. He came in the form of fire. She, accustomed to the ordinary temperature of the clime, only shivered before his approaches. Then he wooed her as a shower of rain and won her heart. Kakal was a divinity much more powerful than Lalala, but malicious to the last degree. He also coveted this woman, who was very beautiful. Kakal's importunities were in vain. In spite, he changed her to a cactus, and rooted her to the ground under the burning sun. The god Lalala was powerless to avert this vengeance; but he took up his abode with the cactus woman, still in the form of a rain shower, and never left her, even in the driest seasons. Thus it happens that the bell-top cactus is an unfailing reservoir of pure cool water.

Long after dark we reached the channel of a vanished stream, and Kilooa led us for several miles along its dry bed. He tethered the panting horses and then dashed into the dense thicket on the bank. A hundred yards of scrambling, and we came to a poor thatched hut. The savage raised both hands above his head and uttered a musical falsetto, not unlike the yodel peculiar to the Valais. This call brought out the occupant of the hut, upon whom Briery flashed the light of his lantern. It was an old woman, hideous beyond the imagination of a dyspeptic's dream.

"*Omanana gelaāl!*" exclaimed Kilooa.

"Hail, holy woman," translated Briery.

Between Kilooa and the holy hag there ensued a long colloquy, respectful on his part, sententious and impatient on hers. Briery listened with eager attention. Several times he clutched my arm, as if unable to repress his anxiety. The woman seemed to be persuaded by Kilooa's arguments, or won by his entreaties. At last she pointed toward the southeast, slowly pronouncing a few words that apparently satisfied my companions.

The direction indicated by the holy woman was still toward the hills, but twenty or thirty degrees to the left of the general course which we had pursued since leaving the shore.

"Push on! Push on!" cried Briery. "We can afford to lose no time."

II

We rode all right. At sunrise there was a pause of hardly ten minutes for the scanty breakfast supplied by our haversacks. Then we were again in the saddle, making our way through a thicket that grew more and more difficult, and under a sun that grew hotter.

"Perhaps," I remarked finally to my taciturn friend, "you have no objection to telling me now why two civilized beings and one amiable savage should be plunging through this infernal jungle, as if they were on an errand of life or death?"

"Yes," said he, "it is best you should know."

Briery produced from an inner breast pocket a letter which had been read and reread until it was worn in the creases. "This," he went on, "is from Professor Quakversuch of the University of Upsala. It reached me in Valparaiso."

Glancing cautiously around, as if he feared that every tree fern in that tropical wilderness was an eavesdropper, or that the hoodlike spathes of the giant caladiums overhead were ears waiting to drink in some mighty secret of science, Briery read in a low voice from the letter of the great Swedish botanist:

"You will have in these islands," wrote the professor, "a rare opportunity to investigate certain extraordinary accounts given me years ago by the Jesuit missionary Buteaux concerning the Migratory Tree, the *cereus vagrans* of Jansenius and other speculative physiologists.

"The explorer Spohr claims to have beheld it; but there is some reason, as you know, for accepting all of Spohr's statements with caution.

"That is not the case with the assertions of my late valued correspondent, the Jesuit missionary. Father Buteaux was a learned botanist, an accurate observer, and a most pious and conscientious man. He never saw the Migratory Tree; but during the long periods of his labors in that part of the world he accumulated, from widely different sources, a mass of testimony as to its existence and habits.

"Is it quite inconceivable, my dear Briery, that somewhere in the range of nature there is a vegetable organization as far above the cabbage, let us say, in complexity and potentiality as the ape is above the polyp? Nature is continuous. In all her schemes we find no chasms, no gaps. There may be missing links in our books and classifications and cabinets, but there are none in the organic world. Is not all of lower nature struggling upward to arrive at the point of self-consciousness and volition? In the unceasing process of evolution, differentiation, improvement in special functions, why may not a plant arrive at this point and feel, will, act, in short, possess and exercise the characteristics of the true animal?"

Briery's voice trembled with enthusiasm as he read this.

"I have no doubt," continued Professor Quakversuch, "that if it shall be your great good fortune to encounter a specimen of the Migratory Tree described by Buteaus, you will find that it possesses a well-defined system of real nerves and ganglia, constituting, in fact, the seat of vegetable intelligence. I conjure you to be very thorough in your dissections.

"According to the indications furnished me by the Jesuit, this extraordinary tree should belong to the order of *Cactaceae*. It should be developed only in conditions of extreme heat and dryness. Its roots should be hardly more than rudimentary, affording a precarious attachment to the earth. This attachment it should be able to sever at will, soaring up into the air and away to another place selected by itself, as a bird shifts its habitation. I infer that these migrations are accomplished by means of the property of secreting hydrogen gas, with which it inflates at pleasure a bladder-like organ of highly elastic tissue, thus lifting itself out of the ground and off to a new abode.

"Buteaux added that the Migratory Tree was invariably worshipped by the natives as a supernatural being, and that the mystery thrown by them around its cult was the greatest obstacle in the path of the investigator."

"There!" exclaimed Briery, folding up Professor Quakversuch's letter. "Is that not a quest worthy the risk or sacrifice of life itself!? To add to the recorded facts of vegetable morphology the proved existence of a tree that wanders, a tree that wills, a tree, perhaps, that thinks—this is glory to be won at any cost! The lamented Decandolle of Geneva—"

"Confound the lamented Decandolle of Geneva!" shouted I, for it was excessively hot, and I felt that we had come on a fool's errand.

III

It was near sunset on the second day of our journey, when Kilooa, who was riding several rods in advance of us, uttered a quick cry, leaped from his saddle, and stooped to the ground.

Briery was at his side in an instant. I followed with less agility; my joints were very stiff, and I had no scientific enthusiasm to lubricate them. Briery was on his hands and knees, eagerly examining what seemed to be a recent disturbance in the soil. The savage was prostrate, rubbing his forehead in the dust, as if in a religious ecstasy, and warbling the same falsetto notes that we had heard at the holy woman's hut.

"What beast's trail have you struck?" I demanded.

"The trail of no beast," answered Briery, almost angrily. "Do you see this broad round abrasion of the surface, where a heavy weight has rested? Do you see these little troughs in the fresh earth, radiating from the center like the points of a star? They are the scars left by slender roots torn up from their shallow beds. Do you see Kilooa's hysterical performance? I tell you we are on the track of the Sacred Tree. It has been here, and not long ago."

Acting under Briery's excited instructions, we continued the hunt on foot. Kilooa started toward the east, I toward the west, and Briery took the southward course.

To cover the ground thoroughly, we agreed to advance in gradually widening zigzags, communicating with each other at intervals by pistol shots. There could have been no more foolish arrangement. In a quarter of an hour I had lost my head and my bearings in a thicket. For another quarter of an hour I discharged my revolver repeatedly, without getting a single response from east or south. I spent the remainder of daylight in a blundering effort to make my way back to the place where the horses were; and then the sun went down, leaving me in sudden darkness, alone in a wilderness of the extent and character of which I had not the faintest idea.

I will spare you the history of my sufferings during the whole of that night, and the next day, and the next night, and another day. When it was dark I wandered about in blind despair, longing for daylight, not daring to sleep or even to stop, and in continual terror of the unknown dangers that surrounded me. In the daytime I longed for night, for the sun scorched its way through the thickest roof that the luxuriant foliage afforded, and drove me nearly mad. The provisions in my haversack were exhausted. My canteen was on my saddle; I should have died of thirst had it not been for the bell-top cactus, which I found twice. But in that horrible experience neither the torture of hunger and thirst nor the torture of heat equaled the misery of the thought that my life was to be sacrificed to the delusion of a crazy botanist, who had dreamed of the impossible.

The impossible?

On the second afternoon, still staggering aimlessly on through the jungle, I lost my last strength and fell to the ground. Despair and indifference had long since given way to an eager desire for the end. I closed my eyes with indescribable relief; the hot sun seemed pleasant on my face as consciousness departed.

Did a beautiful and gentle woman come to me while I lay unconscious, and take my head in her lap, and put her arms around me? Did she press her face to mine and in a whisper bid me have courage? That was the belief that filled my mind when it struggled back for a moment into consciousness; I clutched at the warm, soft arms, and swooned again.

Do not look at each other and smile, gentlemen; in that cruel wilderness, in my helpless condition, I found pity and benignant tenderness. The next time my senses returned I saw that Something *was* bending over me—something majestic if not beautiful, humane if not human, gracious if not woman. The arms that held me and drew me up were moist, and they throbbed with the pulsation of life. There was a faint, sweet odor, like the smell of a woman's perfumed hair. The touch was a caress, the clasp an embrace.

Can I describe its form? No, not with the definiteness that would satisfy the Quakversuches and the Brierys. I saw that the trunk was massive. The branches that lifted me from the ground and held me carefully and gently were flexible and symmetrically disposed. Above my head there was a wreath of strange foliage, and in the midst of it a dazzling sphere of scarlet. The scarlet globe grew while I watched it, but the effort of watching was too much for me.

Remember, if you please, that at this time, physical exhaustion and mental torture had brought me to the point where I passed to and fro between consciousness and unconsciousness as easily and as frequently as one fluctuates between slumber and wakefulness during a night of fever. It seemed the most natural thing in the world that in my extreme weakness I should be beloved and cared for by a cactus. I did not seek an explanation of this good fortune, or try to analyze it; I simply accepted it as a matter of course, as a child accepts a benefit from an unexpected quarter. The one idea that possessed me was that I had found an unknown friend, instinct with womanly sympathy and immeasurably kind.

And as night came on it seemed to me that the scarlet bulb overhead became enormously distended, so that it almost filled the sky. Was I gently rocked by the supple arms that still held me? Were we floating off together into the air? I did not know, or care. Now I fancied that I was in my berth on board ship, cradled by the swell of the sea; now, that I was sharing the flight of some great bird; now, that I was borne on with prodigious speed through the darkness by my own volition. The sense of incessant motion affected all my dreams. Whenever I awoke I felt a cool breeze steadily beating against my face—the first breath of air since we had landed. I was vaguely happy, gentlemen. I had surrendered all responsibility for my own fate. I had gained the protection of a being of superior powers.

IV

"The brandy flask, Kilooa!"

It was daylight. I lay upon the ground and Briery was supporting my shoulders. In his face was a look of bewilderment that I shall never forget.

"My God!" he cried, "and how did you get here? We gave up the search two days ago."

The brandy pulled me together. I staggered to my feet and looked around. The cause of Briery's extreme amazement was apparent at a glance. We were not in the wilderness. We were at the shore. There was the bay, and the ship at anchor, half a mile off. They were already lowering a boat to send for us.

And there to the south was a bright red spot on the horizon, hardly larger than the morning star—the Balloon Tree returning to the wilderness. I saw it, Briery saw it, the savage Kilooa saw it. We watched it till it vanished. We watched it with very different emotions, Kilooa with superstitious reverence, Briery with scientific interest and intense disappointment, I with a heart full of wonder and gratitude.

I clasped my forehead with both hands. It was no dream, then. The Tree, the caress, the embrace, the scarlet bulb, the night journey through the air were not creations and incidents of delirium. Call it tree, or call it plant-animal—there it was! Let men of science quarrel over the question of its existence in nature; this I know: *It had found me dying and had brought me more than a hundred miles straight to the ship where I belonged.* Under Providence, gentlemen, that sentient and intelligent vegetable organism had saved my life.

At this point the colonel got up and left the club. He was very much moved. Pretty soon Briery came in, briskly as usual. He picked up an uncut copy of Lord Bragmuch's *Travels in Kerguellon's Land,* and settled himself in an easy chair at the corner of the fireplace.

Young Traddies timidly approached the veteran globetrotter. "Excuse me, Mr. Briery," he said, "but I should like to ask you a question about the Balloon Tree. Were there scientific reasons for believing that its sex was—"

"Ah," interrupted Briery, looking bored; "the colonel has been favoring you with that extraordinary narrative? Has he honored me again with a share in the adventure? Yes? Well, did we bag the game this time?"

"Why, no," said young Traddies. "You last saw the Tree as a scarlet spot against the horizon."

"By Jove, another miss!" said Briery, calmly beginning to cut the leaves of his book.

The Doom That Came to Sarnath

H. P. LOVECRAFT

Howard Phillips Lovecraft (1890-1937) was an odd and reclusive Rhode Islander who exerted a powerful influence over the fantasy writers of his time, guiding them by correspondence and example. Lovecraft created the "Cthulhu mythos," a body of terrifying fiction dealing with a race of demonic Elder Gods, that he was willing to share with his fellow authors; many collaborated with him on these stories, and so strong was the pull of the Cthulhu legend that new tales in the mythos are still being written, a generation after Lovecraft's death, by writers who had been infants when the original stories were created.

But there was another side to Lovecraft's work–the delicate, haunting stories of vanished lands, not nearly so horrifying as the macabre Cthulhu works. He wrote most of these between 1918 and 1926, but they were not published until many years later, when the fame of his weird tales made possible the publication of some of his more poetic works. "The Doom That Came to Sarnath" is in this group, written in 1919, first published in 1935, a brief glimpse into a land only Lovecraft knew.

There is in the land of Mnar a vast still lake that is fed by no stream, and out of which no stream flows. Ten thousand years ago there stood by its shore the mighty city of Sarnath, but Sarnath stands there no more.

It is told that in the immemorial years when the world was young, before ever the men of Sarnath came to the land of Mnar, another city stood beside the lake; the gray stone city of Ib, which was old as the lake itself, and peopled with beings not pleasing to behold. Very odd and ugly were these beings, as indeed are most beings of a world yet inchoate and rudely fashioned. It is written on the brick cylinders of Kadatheron that the beings of Ib were in hue as green as the lake and the mists that rise above it; that they had bulging eyes, pouting, flabby lips, and curious ears, and were without voice. It is also written that they descended one night from the moon in a mist; they and the vast still lake and gray stone city Ib. However this may be, it is certain that they worshipped a sea-green stone idol chiseled in the likeness of Bokrug, the great water-lizard; before which they danced horribly when the moon was gibbous. And it is written in the papyrus of Ilarnek, that they one day discovered fire, and thereafter kindled flames on many ceremonial occasions. But not much is written of these beings, because they lived in very ancient times, and man is young, and knows but little of the very ancient living things.

After many eons men came to the land of Mnar, dark shepherd folk with their fleecy flocks, who built Thraa, Ilarnek, and Kadatheron on the winding river Ai. And certain tribes, more hardy than the rest, pushed on the border of the lake and built Sarnath at the spot where precious metals were found in the earth.

Not far from the gray city of Ib did the wandering tribes lay the first stones of Sarnath, and at the beings of Ib they marveled greatly. But with their marveling was mixed hate, for they thought it not meet that beings of such aspect should walk about the world of men at dusk. Nor did they like the strange sculptures upon the gray monoliths of Ib, for those sculptures lingered so late in the world, even until the coming men, none can tell; unless it was because the land of Mnar is very still, and remote from other lands, both of waking and of dream.

As the men of Sarnath beheld more of the beings of Ib their hate grew, and it was not less because they found the beings weak, and soft as jelly to the touch of stones and arrows. So one day the young warriors, the slingers and the spearmen and the bowmen, marched against Ib and slew all the inhabitants thereof, pushing the queer bodies into the lake with long spears, because they did not wish to touch them. And because they did not like the gray sculptured monoliths of Ib they cast these also into the lake; wondering from the greatness of the labor how ever the stones were brought from afar, as they must have been, since there is naught like them in the land of Mnar or in the lands adjacent.

Thus of the very ancient city of Ib was nothing spared, save the sea-green stone idol chiseled in the likeness of Bokrug, the water-lizard. This the young warriors took back with them as a symbol of conquest over the old gods and beings of Ib, and as a sign of leadership in Mnar. But on the night after it was set up in the temple, a terrible thing must have happened, for weird lights were seen over the lake, and in the morning the people found the idol gone and the high-priest Taran-Ish lying dead, as from some fear unspeakable. And before he died, Taran-Ish had scrawled upon the altar of chrysolite with coarse shaky strokes the sign of DOOM.

After Taran-Ish there were many high-priests in Sarnath, but never was the sea-green idol found. And many centuries came and went, wherein Sarnath prospered exceedingly, so that only priests and old women remembered what Taran-Ish had scrawled upon the altar of chrysolite. Betwixt Sarnath and the city of Ilarnek arose a caravan route, and the precious metals and rare cloths and jewels and books and tools for artificers and all things of luxury that are known to the people who dwell along the winding river Ai and beyond. So Sarnath waxed mighty and learned and beautiful, and sent forth conquering armies to subdue the neighboring cities; and in time there sat upon a throne in Sarnath the kings of all the land of Mnar and of many lands adjacent.

The wonder of the world and the pride of all mankind was Sarnath the magnificent. Of polished desert-quarried marble were its walls, in height three hundred cubits and in breadth seventy-five, so that chariots might pass each other as men drove them along the top. For full five hundred stadia did they run, being open only on the side toward the lake, where a green stone sea-wall kept back the waves that rose oddly once a year at the festival of the destroying of Ib. In Sarnath were fifty streets from the lake to the gates of the caravans, and fifty more intersecting them. With onyx were they paved, save those whereon the horses and camels and elephants trod, which were paved with granite. And the gates of Sarnath were as many as the landward ends of the streets, each of bronze, and flanked by the figures of lions and elephants carven from some stone no longer known among men. The houses of Sarnath were of glazed brick and chalcedony, each having its walled garden and crystal lakelet. With strange art were they builded, for no other city had houses like them; and travelers from Thraa and Ilarnek and Kadatheron marveled at the shining domes wherewith they were surmounted.

But more marvelous still were the palaces and temples, and the gardens made by Zokkar the olden king. There were many palaces, the last of which were mightier than any in Thraa or Ilarnek or Kadatheron. So high were they that one within might sometimes fancy himself beneath only the sky; yet when lighted with torches dipt in the oil of Dother their walls showed vast paintings of kings and armies, of a splendor at once inspiring and stupefying to the beholder. Many were the pillars of the palaces, all of tinted marble, and carven into designs of surpassing beauty. And in most of the palaces the floors were mosaics of beryl and lapis lazuli and sardonyx and carbuncle and other choice materials, so disposed that the beholder might fancy himself walking over beds of raised flowers. And there were likewise fountains, which cast scented waters about in pleasing jets arranged with cunning art. Outshining all others was the palace of the kings of Mnar and of the lands adjacent. On a pair of golden crouching lions rested the throne, many steps above the gleaming floor. And it was wrought of one piece of ivory, though no man lives who knows whence so vast a piece could have come. In that palace there were also many galleries, and many amphitheaters where lions and men and elephants battled at the pleasure of the kings. Sometimes the amphitheaters were flooded with water conveyed from the lake in mighty aqueducts, and then were enacted stirring sea-fights, or combats betwixt swimmers and deadly marine things.

Lofty and amazing were the seventeen tower-like temples of Sarnath, fashioned of a bright multi-colored stone not known elsewhere. A full thousand cubits high stood the greatest among them, wherein the high-priests dwelt with a magnificence scarce less than that of the kings. On the ground were halls as vast and splendid as those of the palaces; where gathered throngs in worship of Zo-Kalar and Tamash and Lobon, the chief gods of Sarnath, whose incense-enveloped shrines were as the thrones of monarchs. Not like the eikons of other gods were those of Zo-Kalar and Tamash and Lobon. For so close to life were they that one might swear the graceful bearded gods themselves sate on the ivory throne. And up unending steps of zircon was the tower-chamber, wherefrom the high-priests looked out over the city and the plains and the lake by day; and at the cryptic moon and significant stars and planets, and their reflections in the lake, at night. Here was done the very secret and ancient rite of detestation of Bokrug, the water-lizard, and here rested the altar of chrysolite which bore the Doomscrawl of Taran-Ish.

Wonderful likewise were the gardens made by Zokkar the olden king. In the center of Sarnath they lay, covering a great space and encircled by a high wall. And they were surmounted by a mighty dome of glass, through which shone the sun and moon and planets when it was clear; and from which were hung fulgent images of the sun and moon and stars and planets when it was not clear. In summer the gardens were cooled with fresh odorous breezes skillfully wafted by fans, and in winter they were heated with concealed fires, so that in those gardens it was always spring. There ran little streams over bright pebbles, dividing meads of green and gardens of many hues, and spanned by a multitude of bridges. Many were the waterfalls in their courses, and many were the lilied lakelets into which they expanded. Over the streams and lakelets rode white swans, whilst the music of rare birds chimed in with the melody of the waters. In ordered terraces rose the green banks, adorned here and there with bowers of vines and sweet blossoms, and seats and benches of marble and porphyry. And there were many small shrines and temples where one might rest or pray to small gods.

Each year there was celebrated in Sarnath the feast of the destroying of Ib, at which time wine, song, dancing and merriment of every kind abounded. Great honors were then paid to the shades of those who had annihilated the odd ancient beings, and the memory of those beings and of their elder gods was derided by dancers and lutenists crowned with roses from the gardens of Zokkar. And the kings would look out over the lake and curse the bones of the dead that lay beneath it.

At first the high-priests liked not these festivals, for there had descended amongst them queer tales of how the sea-green eikon had vanished, and how Taran-Ish had died from fear and left a warning. And they said that from their high tower they sometimes saw lights beneath the waters of the lake. But as many years passed without calamity, even the priests laughed and cursed and joined in the orgies of the feasters. Indeed, had they not themselves, in their high tower, often performed the very ancient and secret rite in detestation of Bokrug, the water-lizard? And a thousand years of riches and delight passed over Sarnath, wonder of the world.

Gorgeous beyond thought was the feast of the thousandth year of the destroying of Ib. For a decade it had been talked of in

THE DOOM THAT CAME TO SARNATH

the land of Mnar, and as it drew nigh there came to Sarnath on horses and camels and elephants men from Thraa, Ilarnek, and Kadatheron, and all the cities of Mnar and the lands beyond. Before the marble walls on the appointed night were pitched the pavilions of princes and the tents of travelers. Within his banquet-hall reclined Nargis-Hei, the king, drunken with ancient wine from the vaults of conquered Pnoth, and surrounded by feasting nobles and hurrying slaves. There were eaten many strange delicacies at that feast; peacocks from the distant hills of Implan, heels of camels from the Bnazic desert, nuts and spices from Sydathrian groves, and pearls from wave-washed Mtal dissolved in the vinegar of Thraa. Of sauces there were untold number, prepared by the subtlest cooks of all Mnar, and suited to the palate of every feaster. But most prized of all the viands were the great fishes from the lake, each of vast size, and served upon golden platters set with rubies and diamonds.

Whilst the king and his nobles feasted within the palace, and viewed the crowning dish as it awaited them on golden platters, others feasted elsewhere. In the tower of the great temple the priests held revels, and in pavilions without the walls the princes of neighboring lands made merry. And it was the high-priest Gnai-Kah who first saw the shadows that descended from the gibbous moon into the lake, and the damnable green mists that arose from the lake to meet the moon and to shroud in a sinister haze the towers and domes of fated Sarnath. Thereafter those in the towers and without the walls beheld strange lights on the water, and saw that the gray rock Akurion, which was wont to rear high above it near the shore, was almost submerged. And fear grew vaguely yet swiftly, so that the princes of Ilarnek and of far Rokol took down and folded their tents and pavilions and departed, though they scarce knew the reason for their departing.

Then, close to the hour of midnight, all the bronze gates of Sarnath burst open and emptied forth a frenzied throng that blackened the plain, so that all the visiting princes and travelers fled away in fright. For on the faces of this throng was writ a madness born of horror unendurable, and on their tongues were words so terrible that no hearer paused for proof. Men whose eyes were wild with fear shrieked aloud of the sight within the king's banquet-hall, where through the windows were seen no longer the forms of Nargis-Hei and his nobles and slaves, but a horde of indescribable green voiceless things with bulging eyes, pouting, flabby lips, and curious ears; things which danced horribly, bearing in their paws golden platters set with rubies and diamonds, and containing uncouth flames. And the princes and travelers, as they fled from the doomed city of Sarnath on horses and camels and elephants, looked again upon the mist-begetting lake and saw the gray rock Akurion was quite submerged. Through all the land of Mnar and the land adjacent spread the tales of those who had fled from Sarnath, and caravans sought that accursed city and its precious metals no more. It was long ere any travelers went thither, and even then only the brave and adventurous young men of yellow hair and blue eyes, who are no kin to the men of Mnar. These men indeed went to the lake to view Sarnath; but though they found the vast still lake itself, and the gray rock Akurion which rears high about it near the shore, they beheld not the wonder of the world and pride of all mankind. Where once had risen walls of three hundred cubits and towers yet higher, now stretched only the marshy shore, and where once had dwelt fifty million of men now crawled the detestable water-lizard. Not even the mines of precious metal remained. DOOM had come to Sarnath.

But half buried in the rushes was spied a curious green idol; an exceedingly ancient idol chiseled in the likeness of Bokrug, the great water-lizard. That idol, enshrined in the high temple of Ilarnek, was subsequently worshipped beneath the gibbous moon throughout the land of Mnar.

A Tale of the Ragged Mountains

EDGAR ALLEN POE

The term "science fiction" had not been coined, nor would be for decades, when Poe's "A Tale of the Ragged Mountains" was published in 1844. Yet science fiction is indisputably what the story is, for in it Poe attempts a rational and logical explanation of the fantastic and impossible. Although he is generally remembered today for his horror stories, "The Tell-Tale Heart" and "The Black Cat," "The Fall of the House of Usher," and so forth, Poe is regarded by historians of science fiction as one of the founders of the genre, in such stories as "The Facts in the Case of M. Valdemar," "A Descent into the Maelstrom," and the one presented here, an eerie and disturbing account of an adventure in time and space.

During the fall of the year 1827, while residing near Charlottesville, Virginia, I casually made the acquaintance of Mr. Augustus Bedloe. This young gentleman was remarkable in every respect, and excited in me a profound interest and curiosity. I found it impossible to comprehend him either in his moral or his physical relations. Of his family I could obtain no satisfactory account. Whence he came, I never ascertained.

Even about his age—although I call him a young gentleman—there was something which perplexed me in no little degree. He certainly *seemed* young—and he made a point of speaking about his youth—yet there were moments when I should have had little trouble in imagining him a hundred years of age. But in no regard was he more peculiar than in his personal appearance. He was singularly tall and thin. He stooped much. His limbs were exceedingly long and emaciated. His forehead was broad and low. His complexion was absolutely bloodless. His mouth was large and flexible, and his teeth were more wildly uneven, although sound, than I had ever before seen teeth in a human head. The expression of his smile, however, was by no means unpleasing, as might be supposed; but it had no variation whatever. It was one of profound melancholy—of a phaseless and unceasing gloom. His eyes were abnormally large, and round like those of a cat. The pupils, too, upon any accession or diminution of light, underwent contraction or dilation, just such as is observed in the feline tribe. In moments of excitement the orbs grew bright to a degree almost inconceivable; seeming to emit luminous rays, not of a reflected, but of an intrinsic lustre, as does a candle or the sun; yet their ordinary condition was so totally vapid, filmy, and dull, as to convey the idea of the eyes of a long-interred corpse.

These peculiarities of person appeared to cause him much annoyance, and he was continually alluding to them in a sort of half-explanatory, half-apologetic strain, which, when I first heard it, impressed me very painfully. I soon, however, grew accustomed to it, and my uneasiness wore off. It seemed to be his design rather to insinuate than directly to assert that, physically, he had not always been what he was—that a long series of neuralgic attacks had reduced him from a condition of more than usual personal beauty, to that which I saw. For many years past he had been attended by a physician, named Templeton—an old gentleman, perhaps seventy years of age—whom he had first encountered at Saratoga, and from whose attention, while there, he either received, or fancied that he received, great benefit. The result was that Bedloe, who was wealthy, had made an arrangement with Doctor Templeton, by which the latter, in consideration of a liberal annual allowance, had consented to devote his time and medical experience exclusively to the care of the invalid.

Doctor Templeton had been a traveller in his young days, and, at Paris, had become a convert, in great measure, to the doctrines of Mesmer. It was altogether by means of magnetic remedies that he had succeeded in alleviating the acute pains of his patient; and this success had very naturally inspired the latter with a certain degree of confidence in the opinions from which the remedies had been educed. The Doctor, however, like all enthusiasts, had struggled hard to make a thorough convert of his pupil, and finally so far gained his point as to induce the sufferer to submit to numerous experiments.— By a frequent repetition of these, a result had arisen, which of late days has become so common as to attract little or no attention, but which, at the period of which I write, had very rarely been known in America. I mean to say, that between Doctor Templeton and Bedloe there had grown up, little by little, a very distinct and strongly marked rapport, or magnetic relation. I am not prepared to assert, however, that this rapport extended beyond the limits of the simple sleep-producing power; but this power itself had attained great intensity. At the first attempt to induce the magnetic somnolency, the mesmerist entirely failed. In the fifth or sixth he succeeded very partially, and after long continued effort. Only at the twelfth was the triumph complete. After this the will of the patient succumbed rapidly to that of the physician, so that, when I first became acquainted with the two, sleep was brought about almost instantaneously, by the mere volition of the operator, even when the invalid was unaware of his presence. It is only now, in the year 1845, when similar miracles are witnessed daily by thousands, that I dare venture to record this apparent impossibility as a matter of serious fact.

The temperature of Bedloe was, in the highest degree, sensitive, excitable, enthusiastic. His imagination was singularly vigorous and creative; and no doubt it derived additional force from the habitual use of morphine, which he swallowed in great quantity, and without which he would have found it impossible to exist. It was his practice to take a very large dose of it immediately after breakfast, each morning—or rather immediately after a cup of strong coffee, for he ate nothing in the forenoon—and then to set forth alone, or attended only by a dog, upon a long ramble among the chain of wild and dreary hills that lie westward and southward of Charlottesville, and are there dignified by the title of the Ragged Mountains.

Upon a dim, warm, misty day, towards the close of November, and during the strange interregnum of the seasons which in America is termed the Indian Summer, Mr. Bedloe departed as usual, for the hills. The day passed, and still he did not return.

About eight o'clock at night, having become seriously alarmed at his protracted absence, we were about setting out in search of him, when he unexpectedly made his appearance, in health no worse than usual, and in rather more than ordinary spirits. The account which he gave of his expedition, and of the events which had detained him, was a singular one indeed.

"You will remember," said he, "that it was about nine in the morning when I left Charlottesville. I bent my steps immediately to the mountains, and, about ten, entered a gorge which was entirely new to me. I followed the windings of this pass with much interest.— The scenery which presented itself on all sides, although scarcely entitled to be called grand, had about it an indescribable, and to me, a delicious aspect of dreary desolation. The solitude seemed absolutely virgin. I could not help believing that the green sods and the gray rocks upon which I trod, had been trodden never before by the foot of a human being. So entirely secluded, and in fact inaccessible, except through a series of accidents, is the entrance of the ravine, that it is by no means impossible that I was indeed the first adventurer—the very first and sole adventurer who had ever penetrated its recesses.

"The thick and peculiar mist, or smoke, which distinguishes the Indian Summer, and which now hung heavily over all objects, served, no doubt, to deepen the vague impressions which those objects created. So dense was this pleasant fog, that I could at no time see more than a dozen yards of the path before me. This path was excessively sinuous, and as the sun could not be seen, I soon lost all idea of the direction in which I had journeyed. In the meantime the morphine had its customary effect—that of enduing all the external world with an intensity of interest. In the quivering of a leaf—in the hue of a blade of grass—in the shape of a trefoil—in the humming of a bee—in the gleaming of a dew-drop—in the breathing of the wind—in the faint odours that came from the forest—there came a whole universe of suggestion—a gay and motley train of rhapsodical and immethodical thought.

"Busied in this, I walked on for several hours, during which the mist deepened around me to so great an extent, that at length I was reduced to an absolute groping of the way. And now an indescribable uneasiness possessed me—a species of nervous hesitation and tremor.— I feared to tread, lest I should be precipitated into some abyss. I remembered, too, strange stories told about these Ragged Hills, and of the uncouth and fierce races of men who tenanted their groves and caverns. A thousand vague fancies oppressed and disconcerted me—fancies the more distressing because vague. Very suddenly my attention was arrested by the loud beating of a drum.

"My amazement was, of course, extreme. A drum in these hills was a thing unknown. I could not have been more surprised at the sound of the trump of the Archangel. But a new and still more astounding source of interest and perplexity arose. There came a wild rattling or jingling sound, as if of a bunch of large keys—and upon the instant a dusky-visaged and half-naked man rushed past me with a shriek. He came so close to my person that I felt his hot breath upon my face. He bore in one hand an instrument composed of an assemblage of steel rings, and shook them vigorously as he ran. Scarcely had he disappeared in the mist, before, panting after him, with open mouth and glaring eyes, there darted a huge beast. I could not be mistaken in its character. It was a hyena.

"The sight of this monster rather relieved than heightened my terrors—for I now made sure that I dreamed, and endeavored to arouse myself to waking consciousness. I stopped boldly and briskly forward. I rubbed my eyes. I called aloud. I pinched my limbs. A small spring of water presented itself to my view, and here, stooping, I bathed my hands and my head and neck. This seemed to dissipate the equivocal sensations which had hitherto annoyed me. I arose, as I thought, a new man, and proceeded steadily and complacently on my unknown way.

"At length, quite overcome by exertion, and by a certain oppressive closeness of the atmosphere, I seated myself beneath a tree. Presently there came a feeble gleam of sunshine, and the shadow of the leaves of the tree fell faintly but definitely upon the grass. At this shadow I gazed wonderingly for many minutes. Its character stupefied me with astonishment. I looked upward. The tree was a palm.

"I now arose hurriedly, and in a state of fearful agitation— for the fancy that I dreamed would serve me no longer. I saw—I felt that I had perfect command of my senses—and these senses now brought to my soul a world of novel and singular sensation. The heat became all at once intolerable. A strange odour loaded the breeze.— A low continuous murmur, like that arising from a dull, but gently flowing river, came to my ears, intermingled with the peculiar hum of multitudinous human voices.

"While I listened in an extremity of astonishment which I need not attempt to describe, a strong and brief gust of wind bore off the incumbent fog as if by the wand of an enchanter.

"I found myself at the foot of a high mountain, and looking down into a vast plain, through which wound a majestic river. On the margin of this river stood an Eastern-looking city, such as we read of in the Arabian Tales, but of a character even more singular than any there described. From my position, which was far above the level of the town, I could perceive its every nook and corner, as if delineated on a map. The streets seemed innumerable, and crossed each other irregularly in all directions, but were rather long winding alleys than streets, and absolutely swarmed with inhabitants. The houses were wildly picturesque. On every hand was a wilderness of balconies, of verandas, of minarets, of shrines, and fantastically carved oriels. Bazaars abounded; and in these were displayed rich wares in infinite variety and profusion—silks, muslins, the most dazzling cutlery, the most magnificent jewels and gems. Besides these things, were seen, on all sides, banners and palanquins, litters with stately dames close veiled, elephants gorgeously caparisoned, idols grotesquely hewn, drums, banners and gongs, spears, silver and gilded maces. And amid the crowd, and the clamour, and the general intricacy and confusion—amid the million of black and yellow men, turbaned and robed, and of flowing beard, there roamed a countless multitude of holy filleted bulls, while vast legions of the filthy but sacred ape clambered, chattering and shrieking, about the cornices of the mosques, or clung to the minarets and oriels. From the swarming streets to the banks of the river, there descended innumerable flights of steps leading to bathing places, while the river itself seemed to force a passage with difficulty through the vast fleets of deeply burdened ships that far and wide encountered its surface. Beyond the limits of the city arose, in frequent majestic groups, the palm and the cocoa, with other gigantic and weird trees of vast age; and here and there might be seen a field of rice, the thatched hut of a peasant, a tank, a stray temple, a gypsy camp, or a solitary graceful maiden taking her way, with a pitcher upon her head, to the banks of the magnificent river.

"You will say now, of course, that I dreamed; but not so. What I saw—what I heard—what I felt—what I thought—had about it nothing of the unmistakable idiosyncrasy of the dream. All was rigorously self-consistent. At first, doubting that I was really awake, I entered into a series of tests, which soon convinced me that I really was. Now, when one dreams, and, in the dream, suspects that he dreams, the suspicion *never fails to confirm itself,* and the sleeper is almost immediately aroused. Thus Novalis errs not in saying that 'we are near waking when we dream that we dream.' Had the vision occurred to me as I describe it, without my suspecting that it was a dream, then a dream it might absolutely have been, but, occurring as it did, and suspected and tested as it was, I am forced to class it among other phenomena."

"In this I am not sure that you are wrong," observed Mr. Templeton, "but proceed. You arose and descended into the city."

"I arose," continued Bedloe, regarding the Doctor with an air of profound astonishment, "I arose, as you say, and descended into the city. On my way, I fell in with an immense populace, crowding through every avenue, all in the same direction, and exhibiting in every action the wildest excitement. Very suddenly, and by some inconceivable impulse, I became intensely imbued with personal interest in what was going on. I seemed to feel that I had an important part to play, without exactly understanding what it was. Against the crowd which environed me, however, I experienced a deep sentiment of animosity. I shrank from amid them, and, swiftly, by a circuitous path, reached and entered the city. Here all was the wildest tumult and contention. A small party of men, clad in garments half Indian, half European, and officered by gentlemen in a uniform partly British, were engaged, at great odds, with the swarming rabble of the alleys. I joined the weaker party, arming myself with the weapons of a fallen officer, and fighting I knew not whom with the nervous ferocity of despair. We were soon overpowered by numbers, and driven to seek refuge in a species of kiosk. Here we barricaded ourselves, and, for the present, were secure. From a loophole near the summit of the kiosk, I perceived a vast crowd, in furious agitation, surrounding and assaulting a gay palace that overhung the river. Presently, from an upper window of this palace, there descended an effeminate-looking person, by means of a string made of the turbans of his attendants. A boat was at hand, in which he escaped to the opposite bank of the river.

"And now a new object took possession of my soul. I spoke a few hurried but energetic words to my companions, and, having succeeded in gaining a few of them to my purpose, made a frantic sally from the kiosk. We rushed amid the crowd that surrounded it. They retreated, at first, before us. They rallied, fought madly, and retreated again. In the meantime we were borne far from the kiosk, and became bewildered and entangled among the narrow streets of tall overhanging houses, into the recesses of which the sun had never been able to shine. The rabble pressed impetuously upon us, harassing us with their spears, and overwhelming us with flights of arrows. These latter were very remarkable, and resembled in some respects the writhing creese of the Malay. They were made to imitate the body of a creeping serpent, and were long and black, with a poisoned barb. One of them struck me upon the right temple. I reeled and fell. An instantaneous and dreadful sickness seized me. I struggled—I gasped—I died."

"You will hardly persist *now*," I said, smiling, "that the whole of your adventure was not a dream. You are not prepared to maintain that you are dead?"

When I said these words, I of course expected some lively sally from Bedloe in reply; but, to my astonishment, he hesitated, trembled, became fearfully pallid, and remained silent. I looked towards Templeton. He sat erect and rigid in his chair—his teeth chattered, and his eyes were startling from their sockets. "Proceed!" he at length said hoarsely to Bedloe.

"For many minutes," continued the latter, "my sole sentiment—my sole feeling—was that of darkness and nonentity, with the consciousness of death. At length, there seemed to pass a violent and sudden shock through my soul, as of electricity. With it came the sense of elasticity and of light. This latter I felt—not saw. In an instant I seemed to rise from the ground. But I had no bodily, no visible, audible, or palpable presence. The crowd had departed. The tumult had ceased. The city was in comparative repose. Beneath me lay my corpse, with the arrow in my temple, the whole head greatly swollen and disfigured. Even the corpse seemed a matter in which I had no concern. Volition I had none, but appeared to be impelled into motion, and flitted buoyantly out of the city, retracing the circuitous path by which I had entered it. When I had attained the point of the ravine in the mountains, at which I had encountered the hyena, I again experienced a shock as of a galvanic battery; the sense of weight, of volition, of substance, returned. I became my original self, and bent my steps eagerly homewards—but the past had not lost the vividness of the real—and not now, even for an instant, can I compel my understanding to regard it as a dream."

"Nor was it," said Templeton, with an air of deep solemnity, "yet it would be difficult to say how otherwise it should be termed. Let us suppose only, that the soul of the man of to-day is upon the verge of some stupendous psychal discoveries. Let us content ourselves with this supposition. For the rest I have some explanation to make. Here is a water-colour drawing, which I should have shown to you before, but which an unaccountable sentiment of horror has hitherto prevented me from showing."

We looked at the picture which he presented. I saw nothing in it of an extraordinary character; but its effect on Bedloe was prodigious. He nearly fainted as he gazed. And yet it was but a miniature portrait—a miraculously accurate one, to be sure—of his own very remarkable features. At least this was my thought as I regarded it.

"You will perceive," said Templeton, "the date of this picture—it is here, scarcely visible, in this corner—1780. In this year was the portrait taken. It is the likeness of a dead friend—a Mr. Oldeb—to whom I became much attached at Calcutta, during the administration of Warren Hastings. I was then only twenty years old. When I first saw you, Mr. Bedloe, at Saratoga, it was the miraculous similarity which existed between yourself and the painting, which induced me to accost you, to seek your friendship, and to bring about those arrangements which resulted in my becoming your constant companion. In accomplishing this point, I was urged partly, and perhaps principally, by a regretful memory of the deceased, but also, in part, by an uneasy, and not altogether horrorless curiosity respecting yourself.

"In your detail of the vision which presented itself to you amid the hills, you have described, with minutest accuracy, the Indian city of Benares, upon the Holy River. The riots, the combats, the massacre, were the actual events of the insurrection of Cheyte Sing, which took place in 1780, when Hastings was put in imminent peril of his life. The man escaping by the string of turbans was Cheyte Sing himself. The party in the kiosk were sepoys and British officers, headed by Hastings. Of this party I was one, and did all I could to prevent the rash and fatal sally of the officer who fell, in the crowded alleys, by the poisoned arrow of a Bengalee. That officer was my dearest friend. It was Oldeb. You will perceive by these manuscripts" (here the speaker produced a note-book in which several pages appeared to have been freshly written) "that at the very period in which you fancied these things amid the hills, I was engaged in detailing them upon paper here at home."

In about a week after this conversation, the following paragraphs appeared in a Charlottesville paper:

"We have the painful duty of announcing the death of Mr. AUGUSTUS BEDLO, a gentleman whose amiable manners and many virtues have long endeared him to the citizens of Charlottesville.

"Mr. B., for some years past, has been subject to neuralgia, which has often threatened to terminate fatally; but this can be regarded only as the mediate cause of his decease. The proximate cause was one of especial singularity. In an excursion to the Ragged Mountains, a few days since, a slight cold and fever were contracted, attended with great determination of blood to the head. To relieve this, Dr. Templeton resorted to topical bleeding. Leeches were applied to the temples. In a fearfully brief period the patient died, when it appeared that, in the jar containing the leeches, had been introduced, by accident, one of the venomous vermicular sangsues which are now and then found in the neighboring ponds. This creature fastened itself upon a small artery in the right temple. Its close resemblance to the medicinal leech caused the mistake to be overlooked until too late.

"N. B. The poisonous sangsue of Charlottesville may always be distinguished from the medicinal leech by its blackness, and especially by its writhing or vermicular motions, which very nearly resemble those of a snake."

I was speaking with the editor of the paper in question, upon the topic of this remarkable accident, when it occurred to me to ask how it happened that the name of the deceased had been given as Bedlo.

"I presume," said I, "you have authority for this spelling, but I have always supposed the name to be written with an *e* at the end."

"Authority?—no," he replied. "It is a mere typographical error. The name is Bedlo with an *e*, all the world over, and I never knew it to be spelt otherwise in my life."

"Then," said I, mutteringly, as I turned upon my heel, "then indeed has it come to pass that one truth is stranger than fiction—for Bedlo, without the *e*, what is it but Oldeb conversed? And this man tells me it is a typographical error."

Phantas

OLIVER ONIONS

Oliver Onions, who was born in England (1873–1961), grew so weary of his unusual surname that eventually he had his name legally changed to "George Oliver." But it was as Oliver Onions that he published his elegant and eloquent ghost stories, of which the most famous is the terrifying "The Beckoning Fair One," published in his collection Widdershins *in 1911. Out of the same collection comes "Phantas," which is also a ghost story of sorts, but must in addition be considered science fiction: a tale of time-travel, of a strange and perplexing meeting across the centuries.*

> *For barring all pother*
> *With this, or the other,*
> *Still Britons are Lords of the Main.*
> —The Chapter of Admirals

I

As Abel Keeling lay on the galleon's deck, held from rolling down it only by his own weight and the sun-blackened hand that lay outstretched upon the planks, his gaze wandered, but ever returned to the bell that hung, jammed with the dangerous heel-over of the vessel, in the small ornamental belfry immediately abaft the mainmast. The bell was of cast bronze, with half-obliterated bosses upon it that had been the heads of cherubs; but wind and salt spray had given it a thick incrustation of bright, beautiful, lichenous green. It was this color that Abel Keeling's eyes liked.

For wherever else on the galleon his eyes rested they found only whiteness—the whiteness of extreme eld. There were slightly varying degrees in her whiteness; here she was of a white that glistened like salt granules, there of a grayish chalky white, and again her whiteness had the yellowish cast of decay; but everywhere it was the mild, disquieting whiteness of materials out of which the life had departed. Her cordage was bleached as old straw is bleached, and half her ropes kept their shape little more firmly than the ash of a string keeps its shape after the fire has passed; her pallid timbers were white and clean as bones found in sand; and even the wild frankincense with which (for lack of tar, at her last touching of land) she had been pitched had dried to a pale hard gum that sparkled like quartz in her open seams. The sun was yet so pale a buckler of silver through the still white mists that not a cord or timber cast a shadow; and only Abel Keeling's face and hands were black, carked and cinder-black from exposure to his pitiless rays.

The galleon was the *Mary of the Tower,* and she had a frightful list to starboard. So canted was she that her main yard dipped one of its steel sickles into the glassy water, and, had her foremast remained, or more than the broken stump of her bonaventure mizzen, she must have turned over completely. Many days ago they had stripped the main yard of its course, and had passed the sail under the *Mary*'s bottom, in the hope that it would stop the leak. This it had partly done as long as the galleon had continued to glide one way; then, without coming about, she had begun to glide the other, the ropes had parted, and she had dragged the sail after her, leaving a broad tarnish on the silver sea.

For it was broadside that the galleon glided, almost imperceptibly, ever sucking down. She glided as if a loadstone drew her, and, at first, Abel Keeling had thought it was a loadstone, pulling at her iron, drawing her through the pearly mists that lay like facecloths to the water and hid at a short distance the tarnish left by the sail. But later he had known that it was no loadstone drawing her iron. The motion was due—must be due—to the absolute deadness of the calm in that silent, sinister, three-mile-broad waterway. With the eye of his mind he saw that loadstone now as he lay against a gun-truck, all but toppling down the deck. Soon that would happen again which had happened for five days past. He would hear again the chatter of monkeys and the screaming of parrots, the mat of green and yellow weeds would creep in toward the *Mary* over the quicksilver sea, and once more the sheer wall of rock would rise, and the men would run. . . .

But no; the men would not run this time to drop the fenders. There were no men left to do so, unless Bligh was still alive. Perhaps Bligh was still alive. He had walked half-way down the quarter-deck steps a little before the sudden nightfall of the day before, had then fallen and lain for a minute (dead, Abel Keeling had supposed, watching him from his place by the gun-truck), and had then got up again and tottered forward to the forecastle, his tall figure swaying and his long arms waving. Abel Keeling had not seen him since. Most likely, he had died in the forecastle during the night. If he had not been dead he would have come aft again for water. . . .

At the remembrance of the water Abel Keeling lifted his head. The strands of lean muscle about his emaciated mouth worked, and he made a little pressure of his sun-blackened hands on the deck, as if to verify its steepness and his own balance. The mainmast was some seven or eight yards away. He put one stiff leg under him and began, seated as he was, to make shuffling movements down the slope.

To the mainmast, near the belfry, was affixed his contrivance for catching water. It consisted of a collar of rope set lower at one side than at the other (but that had been before the mast had steeved so many degrees away from the zenith), and tallowed beneath. The mists lingered later in that gulley of a strait than they did on the open ocean, and the collar of rope served as a collector for the dews that condensed on the masts. The drops fell into a small earthen pipkin placed on the deck beneath it.

Abel Keeling reached the pipkin and looked into it. It was nearly a third full of fresh water. Good. If Bligh, the mate, was dead, so much the more water for Abel Keeling, master of the *Mary of the Tower*. He dipped two fingers into the pipkin and put them into his mouth. This he did several times. He did not dare to raise the pipkin to his black and broken lips for dread of a remembered agony, he could not have told how many days ago, when a devil had whispered to him, and he had gulped down the contents of the pipkin in the morning, and for the rest of the day had gone waterless. . . . Again he moistened his fingers and sucked them; then he lay sprawling against the mast, idly watching the drops of water as they fell.

It was odd how the drops formed. Slowly they collected at the edge of the tallowed collar, trembled in their fullness for an instant, and fell, another beginning the process instantly. It amused Abel Keeling to watch them. Why (he wondered) were all the drops the same size? What cause and compulsion did they obey that they never varied, and what frail tenuity held the little globules intact? It must be due to some Cause. . . . He remembered that the aromatic gum of the wild frankincense with which they had parcelled the seams had hung on the buckets in great sluggish gouts, obedient to a different compulsion; oil was different again, and so were juices and balsams. Only quicksilver (perhaps the heavy and motionless sea put him in mind of quicksilver) seemed obedient to no law. . . . Why was it so?

Bligh, of course, would have had his explanation: it was the Hand of God. That sufficed for Bligh, who had gone forward the evening before, and whom Abel Keeling now seemed vaguely and at a distance to remember as the deep-voiced fanatic who had sung his hymns as, man by man, he had committed the bodies of the ship's company to the deep. Bligh was that sort of man; accepted things without question; was content to take things as they were and be ready with the fenders when the wall of rock rose out of the opalescent mists. Bligh, too, like the waterdrops, had his Law, that was his and nobody else's. . . .

There floated down from some rotten rope up aloft a flake of scurf, that settled in the pipkin. Abel Keeling watched it dully as it settled toward the pipkin's rim. When presently he again dipped his fingers into the vessel the water ran into a little vortex, drawing the flake with it. The water settled again; and again the minute flake determined toward the rim and adhered there, as if the rim had power to draw it. . . .

It was exactly so that the galleon was gliding toward the wall of rock, the yellow and green weeds, and the monkeys and parrots. Put out into mid-water again (while there had been men to put her out) she had glided to the other wall. One force drew the chip in the pipkin and the ship over the tranced sea. It was the Hand of God, said Bligh. . . .

Abel Keeling, his mind now noting minute things and now clouded with torpor, did not at first hear a voice that was quakingly lifted up over by the forecastle—a voice that drew nearer, to an accompaniment of swirling water.

> *Oh, Thou, that Jonas in the fish*
> *Three days didst keep from pain,*
> *Which was a figure of Thy death*
> *And rising up again—*

It was Bligh, singing one of his hymns:

> *Oh, Thou, that Noah keptst from flood,*
> *And Abram, day by day,*
> *As he along through Egypt passed*
> *Didst guide him in the way—*

The voice ceased, leaving the pious period uncompleted. Bligh was alive, at any rate. . . . Abel Keeling resumed his fitful musing.

Yes, that was the Law of Bligh's life, to call things the Hand of God; but Abel Keeling's Law was different; no better, no worse, only different. The Hand of God, that drew ships and galleons, must work by some method; and Abel Keeling's eyes were dully on the pipkin again as if he sought the message there. . . .

Then conscious thought left him for a space, and when he resumed it was without obvious connection.

Oars, of course, were the thing. With oars, men could laugh at calms. Oars, that only pinnaces and galleasses now used, had had their advantages. But oars (which was to say a method, for you could say if you liked the Hand of God grasped the oar-loom, as the Breath of God filled the sail)—oars were antiquated, belonging to the past, and meant a throwing-over of all that was good and new and a return to fine lines, a battle formation abreast to give effect to the shock of the ram, and a day or two at sea and then to port again for provisions. Oars . . . no. Abel Keeling was one of the new men, the men who swore by the line-head, the broadside fire of sakers and demi-cannon, and weeks and months without a landfall. Perhaps one day the wits of such men as he would devise a craft, not oar-driven (because oars could not penetrate into the remote seas of the world)—not sail-driven (because men who trusted to sails found themselves in an airless, three-mile strait, suspended motionless between cloud and water, ever gliding to a wall of rock)—but a ship . . . a ship . . .

> *To Noah and his sons with him*
> *God spake, and thus said He:*
> *A cov'nant set I up with you*
> *And your posterity—*

It was Bligh again, wandering somewhere in the waist. Abel

Keeling's mind was once more a blank. Then slowly, slowly, as the water drops collected on the collar of rope, his thought took shape again.

A galleasse? No, not a galleasse. The galleasse made shift to be two things, and was neither. This ship, that the hand of man should one day make for the Hand of God to manage, should be a ship that should take and conserve the force of the wind, take it and store it as she sorted her victuals; at rest when she wished, going ahead when she wished; turning the forces both of calm and storm against themselves. For, of course, her force must be wind—stored wind—a bag of the winds, as the children's tale had it—wind probably directed upon the water astern, driving it away and urging forward the ship, acting by reaction. She would have a wind-chamber, into which wind would be pumped by pumps . . . Bligh would call that equally the Hand of God, this driving force of the ship of the future that Abel Keeling dimly foreshadowed as he lay between the mainmast and the belfry, turning his eyes now and then from the ashy white timbers to the vivid green bronze-rust of the bell above him. . . .

Bligh's face, liver-colored with the sun and ravaged from inward by the faith that consumed him, appeared at the head of the quarter-deck steps. His voice beat uncontrolledly out.

And in the earth here is no place
Of refuge to be found,
Nor in the deep and water-course
That passeth under ground—

II

Bligh's eyes were lidded, as if in contemplation of his inner ecstasy. His head was thrown back, and his brows worked up and down tormentedly. His wide mouth remained open as his hymn was suddenly interrupted on the long-drawn note. From somewhere in the shimmering mists the note was taken up, and there drummed and rang and reverberated through the strait a windy, hoarse, and dismal bellow, alarming and sustained. A tremor rang through Bligh. Moving like a sightless man, he stumbled forward from the head of the quarter-deck steps, and Abel Keeling was aware of his gaunt figure behind him, taller for the steepness of the deck. As that vast empty sound died away, Bligh laughed in his mania.

"Lord, hath the grave's wide mouth a tongue to praise Thee? Lo, again—"

Again the cavernous sound possessed the air, louder and nearer. Through it came another sound, a slow throb, throb—throb, throb—Again the sounds ceased.

"Even Leviathan lifted up his voice in praise!" Bligh sobbed.

Abel Keeling did not raise his head. There had returned to him the memory of the day when, before the morning mists had lifted from the strait, he had emptied the pipkin of the water that was the allowance until night should fall again. During that agony of thirst he had seen shapes and heard sounds with other than his mortal eyes and ears, and even in the moments that had alternated with his lightness, when he had known these to be hallucinations, they had come again. He had heard the bells on a Sunday in his own Kentish home, the calling of children at play, the unconcerned singing of men at their daily labor, and the laughter and gossip of the women as they had spread the linen on the hedge or distributed bread upon the platters. These voices had rung in his brain; interrupted now and then by the groans of Bligh and of two other men who had been alive then. Some of the voices he had heard had been silent on earth this many a long year, but Abel Keeling, thirst-tortured, had heard them, even as he was now hearing that vacant moaning with the intermittent throbbing that filled the strait with alarm. . . .

"Praise Him, praise Him, praise Him!" Bligh was calling deliriously.

Then a bell seemed to sound in Abel Keeling's ears, and, as if something in the mechanism of his brain had slipped, another picture rose in his fancy—the scene when the *Mary of the*

Tower had put out, to a bravery of swinging bells and shrill fifes and valiant trumpets. She had not been a leper-white galleon then. The scroll-work on her prow had twinkled with gilding; her belfry and stern galleries and elaborate lanterns had flashed in the sun with gold; and her fighting-tops and the warpavesse about her waist had been gay with painted coats and scutcheons. To her sails had been stitched gaudy ramping lions of scarlet say, and from her mainyard, now dipping in the water, had hung the two-tailed pennant with the Virgin and Child embroidered upon it. . . .

Then suddenly a voice about him seemed to be saying, "*And a half-seven—and a half-seven—*" and in a twink the picture in Abel Keeling's brain changed again. He was at home again, instructing his son, young Abel, in the casting of the lead from the skiff they had pulled out of the harbor.

"*And a half-seven!*" the boy seemed to be calling.

Abel Keeling's blackened lips muttered: "Excellently well cast, Abel, excellently well cast!"

"*And a half-seven—and a half-seven—seven—seven—*"

"Ah," Abel Keeling murmured, "that last was not a clear cast—give me the line—thus it should go . . . ay, so. . . . Soon you shall sail the seas with me in the *Mary of the Tower*. You are already perfect in the stars and the motions of the planets; tomorrow I will instruct you in the use of the backstaff. . . . "

For a minute or two he continued to mutter; then he dozed. When again he came to semi-consciousness it was once more to the sound of bells, at first faint, then louder, and finally becoming a noisy clamor immediately above his head. It was Bligh. Bligh, in a fresh attack of delirium, had seized the bell lanyard and was ringing the bell insanely. The cord broke in his fingers, but he thrust at the bell with his hand, and again called aloud.

"Upon a harp and an instrument of ten strings . . . let Heaven and Earth praise Thy Name! . . . "

He continued to call aloud, and to beat on the bronze-rusted bell.

"*Ship ahoy! What ship's that?*"

One would have said that a veritable hail had come out of the mists, but Abel Keeling knew those hails that came out of mists. They came from ships which were not there. "Ay, ay, keep a good lookout, and have a care to your lodemanage," he muttered again to his son. . . .

But, as sometimes a sleeper sits up in his dream, or rises from his couch and walks, so all of a sudden Abel Keeling found himself on his hands and knees on the deck, looking back over his shoulder. In some deep-seated region of his consciousness he was dimly aware that the cant of the deck had become more perilous, but his brain received the intelligence and forgot it again. He was looking out into the bright and baffling mists. The buckler of the sun was of a more ardent silver; the sea below it was lost in brilliant evaporation; and between them, suspended in the haze, no more substantial than the vague darknesses that float before dazzled eyes, a pyramidal phantom-shape hung. Abel Keeling passed his hand over his eyes, but when he removed it the shape was still there, gliding slowly towards the *Mary's* quarter. Its form changed as he watched it. The spirit-gray shape that had been a pyramid seemed to dissolve into four upright members, slightly graduated in tallness, that nearest the *Mary's* stern the tallest and that to the left the lowest. It might have been the shadow of the gigantic set of reed-pipes on which that vacant mournful note had been sounded.

And as he looked, with fooled eyes, again his ears became fooled:

"*Ahoy there! What ship's that? Are you a ship? . . . Here, give me that trumpet—*" Then a metallic barking. "*Ahoy there! What the devil are you? Didn't you ring a bell? Ring it again, or blow a blast or something, or go dead slow!*"

All this came, as it were, indistinctly, and through a sort of high singing in Abel Keeling's own ears. Then he fancied a short bewildered laugh, followed by a colloquy from somewhere between sea and sky.

"Here, Ward, just pinch me, will you? Tell me what you see there. I want to know if I'm awake."

"See where?"

"There, on the starboard bow. (Stop that ventilating fan, I can't hear myself think.) See anything? Don't tell me it's that damned Dutchman—don't pitch me that old Vanderdecken tale—give me an easy one first, something about a sea-serpent. . . . You did hear that bell, didn't you?"

"Shut up a minute—listen—"

Again Bligh's voice was lifted up.

> *This is the cov'nant that I make:*
> *From henceforth nevermore*
> *Will I again the world destroy*
> *With water, as before.*

Bligh's voice died away again in Abel Keeling's ears.

"*Oh—my—fat—Aunt—Julia!*" The voice that seemed come between sea and sky sounded again. Then it spoke once more loudly. "*I say*," it began with careful politeness, "*if you are a ship, do you mind telling us where the masquerade is to be? Our wireless is out of order, and we hadn't heard of it. . . . Oh, you do see it, Ward, don't you? . . . Please, please tell us what the hell you are!*"

Again Abel Keeling had moved as a sleepwalker moves. He had raised himself up by the belfry timbers, and Bligh had sunk in a heap on the deck. Abel Keeling's movement overturned the pipkin, which raced the little trickle of its contents down the deck and lodged where the still and brimming sea made, as it were, a chain with the carved balustrade of the quarter-deck— one link a still gleaming edge, then a dark baluster, then another gleaming link. For one moment only Abel Keeling found himself noticing that that which had driven Bligh aft had been the rising of the water in the waist as the galleon settled by the head—the waist was now entirely submerged; then once more he was absorbed in his dream, its voices, and its shape in the mist, which had again taken the form of a pyramid before his eyes.

"*Of course*," a voice seemed to be complaining anew, and still through that confused dinning in Abel Keeling's ears, "*we can't turn a four-inch on it.... And, of course, Ward, I don't believe in 'em. D'you hear, Ward? I don't believe in 'em, I say. ... Shall we call down to old A.B.? This might interest His Scientific Skippership....*"

"*Oh, lower a boat and pull out to it—into it—over it—through it—*"

"*Look at our chaps crowded on the barbette yonder. They've seen it. Better not give an order you know won't be obeyed....*"

Abel Keeling, cramped against the antique belfry, had begun to find his dream interesting. For, though he did not know her build, that mirage was in the shape of a ship. No doubt it was projected from his brooding on ships of half an hour before; and that was odd.... But perhaps, after all, it was not very odd. He knew that she did not really exist; only the appearance of her existed; but things had to exist like that before they really existed. Before the *Mary of the Tower* had existed she had been a shape in some man's imagination; before that, some dreamer had dreamed the form of a ship with oars; and before that, far away in the dawn and infancy of the world, some seer had seen in a vision the raft before man had ventured to push out over the water on his two planks. And since this shape that rode before Abel Keeling's eyes was a shape in his, Abel Keeling's dream, he, Abel Keeling, was the master of it. His own brooding brain had contrived her, and she was launched upon the illimitable ocean of his own mind....

> *And I will not unmindful be*
> *Of this, My cov'nant, passed*
> *Twixt Me and you and every flesh*
> *Whiles that the world should last,*

sang Bligh, rapt....

But as a dreamer, even in his dreams, will scratch upon the wall by his couch some key or word to put him in mind of his vision on the morrow when it has left him, so Abel Keeling found himself seeking some sign to be a proof to those to whom no vision is vouchsafed. Even Bligh sought that—could not be silent in his bliss, but lay on the deck there, uttering great passionate Amens and praising his Maker, as he said, upon a harp and an instrument of ten strings. So with Abel Keeling. It would be the Amen of his life to have praised God, not upon a harp, but upon a ship that should carry her own power, that should store wind or its equivalent as she stored her victuals, that should be something wrested from the chaos of uninvention and ordered and disciplined and subordinated to Abel Keeling's will. . . . And there she was, that ship-shaped thing of spirit-gray, with the four pipes that resembled a phantom organ now broadside and of equal length. And the ghost-crew of that ship were speaking again. . . .

The interrupted silver chain by the quarter-deck balustrade had now become continuous, and the balusters made a herringbone over their own motionless reflections. The spilt water from the pipkin had dried, and the pipkin was not to be seen. Abel Keeling stood beside the mast, erect as God made man to go. With his leathery hand he smote upon the bell. He waited for a space of a minute, and then cried:

"Ahoy! . . . Ship ahoy! . . . What ship's that?"

III

We are not conscious in a dream that we are playing a game the beginning and end of which are in ourselves. In this dream of Abel Keeling's a voice replied:

"*Hallo, it's found its tongue. . . . Ahoy there! What are you?*"

Loudly and in a clear voice Abel Keeling called: "Are you a ship?"

With a nervous giggle the answer came:

"*We are a ship, aren't we, Ward? I hardly feel sure. . . .*"

Yes, of course, we're a ship. No question about us. The question is what the dickens you are."

Not all the words these voices used were intelligible to Abel Keeling, and he knew not what it was in the tone of these last words that reminded him of the honor due to the *Mary of the Tower*. Blister-white and at the end of her life as she was, Abel Keeling was still jealous of her dignity; the voice had a youngish ring; and it was not fitting that young chins should be wagged about his galleon. He spoke curtly.

"You that spoke—are you the master of that ship?"

"*Officer of the watch,*" the words floated back; "*the captain's below.*"

"Then send for him. It is with masters that masters hold speech," Abel Keeling replied.

He could see the two shapes, flat and without relief, standing on a high narrow structure with rails. One of them gave a low whistle, and seemed to be fanning his face; but the other rumbled something into a sort of funnel. Presently the two shapes became three. There was a murmuring, as of a consultation, and then suddenly a new voice spoke. At its thrill and tone a sudden tremor ran through Abel Keeling's frame. He wondered what response it was that that voice found in the forgotten recesses of his memory. . . .

"*Ahoy!*" seemed to call this new yet faintly remembered voice. "*What's all this about? Listen. We're His Majesty's destroyer* Seapink, *out of Devonport last October, and nothing particular the matter with us. Now who are you?*"

"The *Mary of the Tower,* out of the Port of Rye on the day of Saint Anne, and only two men—"

A gasp interrupted him.

"*Out of where?*" that voice that so strangely moved Abel Keeling said unsteadily, while Bligh broke into groans of renewed rapture.

"Out of the Port of Rye, in the Country of Sussex . . . nay, give ear, else I cannot make you hear me while this man's spirit and flesh wrestle so together! . . . Ahoy! Are you gone?" For the voices had become a low murmur, and the ship shape had faded before Abel Keeling's eyes. Again and again he called. He wished to be informed of the disposition and economy of the wind-chamber. . . .

"The wind-chamber!" he called, in an agony lest the knowledge almost within his grasp should be lost. "I would know about the wind-chamber. . . . "

Like an echo, there came back the words, uncomprehendingly uttered, *"The wind-chamber? . . . "*

" . . . that driveth the vessel—perchance 'tis not wind—a steel bow that is bent also conserveth force—the force you store, to move at will through calm and storm. . . . "

"Can you make out what it's driving at?"

"Oh, we shall all wake up in a minute. . . . "

"Quiet, I have it; the engines; it wants to know about our engines. It'll be wanting to see our papers presently. Rye Port! . . . Well, no harm in humoring it; let's see what it can make of this. Ahoy there!" came the voice to Abel Keeling, a little strongly, as if a shifting wind carried it, and speaking faster and faster as it went on. *"Not wind, but steam; d'you hear? Steam, steam. Steam, in eight Yarrow water-tube boilers. S-t-e-a-m, steam. Got it? And we've twin-screw triple expansion engines, indicated horsepower four thousand, and we can do 430 revolutions per minute; savvy? Is there anything your phantomhood would like to know about our armament? . . . "*

Abel Keeling was muttering fretfully to himself. It annoyed him that words in his own vision should have no meaning for him. How did words come to him in a dream that he had no knowledge of when wide awake? The *Seapink*—that was the name of this ship; but a pink was long and narrow, low-cargoed, and square-built aft. . . .

"And as for our armament," the voice with the tones that so profoundly troubled Abel Keeling's memory continued, *"we've two revolving Whitehead torpedo-tubes, three six-pounders on the upper deck, and that's a twelve-pounder forward there by the conning-tower. I forgot to mention that*

we're nickel steel, with a coal capacity of sixty tones in most damnably placed bunkers, and that thirty and a quarter knots is about our top. Care to come aboard?"

But the voice was speaking still more rapidly and feverishly, as if to fill a silence with no matter what, and the shape that uttered it was straining forward anxiously over the rail.

"Ugh! But I'm glad this happened in daylight," another voice was muttering.

"I wish I was sure it was happening at all. . . . Poor old spook!"

"I suppose it would keep its feet if her deck was quite vertical. Think she'll go down, or just melt?"

"Kind of go down . . . without wash. . . ."

"Listen—here's the other one now—"

For Bligh was singing again:

> For, Lord, Thou know'st our nature such
> If we great things obtain
> And in the getting of the same
> Do feel no grief or pain,
>
> We little do esteem thereof;
> But, hardly brought to pass,
> A thousand times we do esteem
> More than the other was.

"But oh, look—look—look at the other! Oh, I say, wasn't he a grand old boy! Look!"

For, transfiguring Abel Keeling's form as a prophet's form is transfigured in the instant of his rapture, flooding his brain with the white eureka-light of perfect knowledge, that for which he and his dream had been at a standstill had come. He knew her, this ship of the future, as if God's Finger had bitten her lines into his brain. He knew her as those already sinking into the grave know things, miraculously, completely, accepting Life's impossibilities with a nodded "Of course." From the ardent mouths of her eight furnaces to the last drip from her lubricators, from her bedplates to the breeches of her quick-firers, he knew her—read her gauges, thumbed her bearings, gave the ranges from her range-finders, and lived the life he lived who was in command of her. And he would not forget on the morrow, as he had forgotten so many morrows, for at last he had seen the water about his feet, and knew that there would be no morrow for him in this world. . . .

And even in that moment, with but a sand or two to run in his glass, indomitable, insatiable, dreaming dream on dream, he could not die until he knew more. He had two questions to ask, and a master-question; and but a moment remained. Sharply his voice rang out.

"Ho, there! . . . This ancient ship, the *Mary of the Tower*, cannot steam thirty and a quarter knots, but yet she can sail the waters. What more does your ship? Can she soar above them, as the fowls of the air soar?"

"*Lord, he thinks we're an aeroplane! . . . No, she can't. . . .*"

"And you can dive, even as the fishes of the deep?"

"*No. . . . Those are submarines . . . we aren't a submarine. . . .*"

But Abel Keeling waited for no more. He gave an exulting chuckle.

"Oho, oho—thirty knots, and but on the face of the waters—no more than that? Oho! . . . Now *my* ship, the ship I see as a mother sees full-grown the child she has but conceived—*my* ship I say—oho, *my* ship. . . . Below there, trip that gun!"

The cry came suddenly and alertly, as a muffled sound came from below and an ominous tremor shook the galleon.

"*By Jove, her guns are breaking loose below—that's her finish—*"

"Trip that gun, and double-breech the others!" Abel Keeling's voice rang out, as if there had been any to obey him. He had braced himself within the belfry frame; and then in the middle of the next order his voice suddenly failed him. His ship shape, that for the moment he had forgotten, rode once more before his eyes. This was the end, and his master-question, apprehension for the answer to which was now torturing his face and well nigh bursting his heart, was still unasked.

"Ho—he that spoke with me—the master," he cried in a voice that ran high, "is he there?"

"*Yes, yes!*" came the other voice across the water, sick with suspense. "*Oh, be quick!*"

There was a moment in which hoarse cries from many voices, a heavy thud and rumble on wood, and a crash of timbers and a gurgle and a splash were indescribably mingled; the gun under which Abel Keeling had lain had snapped her rotten breechings and plunged down the deck, carrying Bligh's unconscious form with it. The deck came up vertical, and for one instant longer Abel Keeling clung to the belfry.

"I cannot see your face," he screamed, "but meseems your voice is a voice I know. *What is your name?*"

"*Keeling—Abel Keeling—oh, my God!*"

And Abel Keeling's cry of triumph, that mounted to a victorious "Huzza!" was lost in the downward plunge of the *Mary of the Tower,* that left the strait empty save for the sun's fiery blaze and the last smoke-like evaporation of the mists.

Trips

ROBERT SILVERBERG

One of the favorite concepts of science-fiction writers is that of the alternate universe—the notion that an infinity of worlds similar to ours lies just beyond our reach, across some barrier of dimensions. If we could only reach some of those worlds, what strangeness, what wonders, what novelties we would behold! It is a lovely fantasy, impossible to prove or disprove. What would it be like to make a voyage through the universes adjoining our own? To go onward, ever onward, through world after world, each one somewhat like our own, and yet so different, so very different. . . .

> Does this path have a heart? All paths are the same: they lead nowhere. They are paths going through the bush, or into the bush. In my own life I could say I have traversed long, long paths, but I am not anywhere. . . . Does this path have a heart? If it does, the path is good; if it doesn't, it is of no use. Both paths lead nowhere; but one has a heart, the other doesn't. One makes for a joyful journey; as long as you follow it, you are one with it. The other will make you curse your life.
> —*The Teachings of Don Juan*

I

The second place you come to—the first having proved unsatisfactory, for one reason and another—is a city which could almost be San Francisco. Perhaps it is, sitting out there on the peninsula between the ocean and the bay, white buildings clambering over improbably steep hills. It occupies the place in your psychic space that San Francisco has always occupied, although you don't really know yet what this city calls itself. Perhaps you'll find out before long.

You go forward. What you feel first is the strangeness of the familiar, and then the utter heartless familiarity of the strange. For example the automobiles, and there are plenty of them, are all halftracks: low sleek sexy sedans that have the flashy Detroit styling, the usual chrome, the usual streamlining, the low-raked windows all agleam, but there are only two wheels, both of them in front, with a pair of tread-belts circling endlessly in back. Is this good design for city use? Who knows? Somebody evidently thinks so, here. And then the newspapers: the format is the same, narrow columns, gaudy screaming headlines, miles of black type on coarse grayish-white paper, but the names and the places have been changed. You scan the front page of a newspaper in the window of a curbside vending machine. Big photo of Chairman DeGrasse, serving as host at a reception for the Patagonian Ambassador. An account of the tribal massacres in the highlands of Dzungaria. Details of the solitude epidemic that is devastating Persepolis. When the halftracks stall on the hillsides, which is often, the other drivers ring silvery chimes, politely venting their impatience. Men who look like Navahos chant what sound like sutras in the intersections. The traffic lights are blue and orange. Clothing tends toward the prosaic, grays and dark blues, but the cut and slope of men's jackets has an angular, formal eighteenth-century look, verging on pomposity. You pick up a bright coin that lies in the street: it is vaguely metallic but rubbery, as if you could compress it between your fingers, and its thick edges bear incuse lettering: TO GOD WE OWE OUR SWORDS. On the next block a squat two-story building is ablaze, and agitated clerks do a desperate dance. The fire engine is glossy green and its pump looks like a diabolical cannon embellished with sweeping flanges; it spouts a glistening yellow foam that eats the flames and, oxidizing, runs off down the gutter, a trickle of sluggish blue fluid. Everyone wears eyeglasses here, *everyone*. At a sidewalk café, pale waitresses offer mugs of boiling-hot milk into which the silent tight-faced patrons put cinnamon, mustard, and what seems to be Tabasco sauce. You offer your coin and try a sample, imitating what they do, and everyone bursts into laughter. The girl behind the counter pushes a thick stack of paper currency at you by way of change: UNITED FEDERAL COLUMBIAN REPUBLIC, each bill declares. GOOD FOR ONE EXCHANGE. Illegible signatures. Portrait of early leader of the republic, so famous that they give him no label of identification, bewigged, wall-eyed, ecstatic. You sip your milk, blowing gently. A light scum begins to form on its speckled surface. Sirens start to wail. About you, the other milk-drinkers stir uneasily. A parade is coming. Trumpets, drums, far-off chanting. Look! Four naked boys carry an open brocaded litter on which there sits an immense block of ice, a great frosted cube, mysterious, impenetrable. "Patagonia!" the onlookers cry sadly. The word is wrenched from them: "Patagonia!" Next, marching by himself, a mitred bishop advances, all in green, curtseying to the crowd, tossing hearty blessings as though they were flowers. "Forget your sins! Cancel your debts! All is made new! All is good!" You shiver and peer intently into his eyes as he passes you, hoping that he will single you out for an embrace. He is terribly tall but white-haired and fragile, somehow, despite his agility and energy. He reminds you of Norman, your wife's older brother, and perhaps he *is* Norman, the Norman of this place, and you wonder if he can give you news of Elizabeth, the Elizabeth of this place, but you say nothing and he goes by. And then comes a tremendous wooden scaffold on wheels, a true juggernaut, at the summit of which rests a polished statue carved out of gleaming black stone: a human figure, male, plump, arms intricately folded, face complacent. The statue emanates a sense of vast Sumerian calm. The face is that of Chairman DeGrasse. "He'll die in the first blizzard," murmurs a man to your left. Another, turning suddenly, says with great force, "No, it's going to be done the proper way. He'll last until the time of the accidents, just as he's supposed to. I'll bet on that." Instantly they are nose to nose, glaring, and then they are wagering—a tense complicated ritual involving slapping of palms, interchanges of slips of paper, formal voiding of spittle, hysterical appeals to witnesses. The emotional climate here seems a trifle too intense. You decide to move along. Warily you leave the café, looking in all directions.

II

Before you began your travels you were told how essential it was to define your intended role. Were you going to be a tourist, or an explorer, or an infiltrator? Those are the choices that confront anyone arriving at a new place. Each bears its special risks.

To opt for being a tourist is to choose the easiest but most contemptible path; ultimately it's the most dangerous one, too, in a certain sense. You have to accept the built-in epithets that go with the part: they will think of you as a *foolish* tourist, an *ignorant* tourist, a *vulgar* tourist, a *mere* tourist. Do you want to be considered mere? Are you able to accept that? Is that really your preferred self-image—baffled, bewildered, led about by the nose? You'll sign up for packaged tours, you'll carry guidebooks and cameras, you'll go to the cathedral and the museums and the marketplace, and you'll remain always on the outside of things, seeing a great deal, experiencing nothing. What a waste! You will be diminished by the very traveling that you thought would expand you. Tourism hollows and parches you. All places become one: a hotel, a smiling swarthy sunglassed guide, a bus, a plaza, a fountain, a marketplace, a museum, a cathedral. You are transformed into a feeble shriveled thing made out of glued-together travel folders; you are naked but for your visas; the sum of your life's adventures is a box of left-over small change from many indistinguishable lands.

To be an explorer is to make the *macho* choice. You swagger in, bent on conquest, for isn't any discovery a kind of conquest? Your existential position, like that of any mere tourist, lies outside the heart of things, but you are unashamed of that; and while tourists are essentially passive, the explorer's role is active; an explorer intends to grasp that heart, take possession, squeeze. In the explorer's role you consciously cloak yourself in the trappings of power: self-assurance, thick bankroll, stack of credit cards. You capitalize on the glamour of being a stranger. Your curiosity is invincible; you ask unabashed questions about the most intimate things, never for an instant relinquishing eye-contact. You open locked doors and flash bright lights into curtained rooms. You are Magellan; you are Malinowski; you are Captain Cook. You will gain much, but—ah, here is the price!—you will always be feared and hated, you will never be permitted to attain the true core. Nor is superficiality the worst peril. Remember that Magellan and Captain Cook left their bones on tropic beaches. Sometimes the natives lose patience with explorers.

The infiltrator, though? His is at once the most difficult role and the most rewarding one. Will it be yours? Consider. You'll have to get right with it when you reach your destination, instantly learn the regulations, find your way around like an old hand, discover the location of shops and freeways and hotels, figure out the units of currency, the rules of social intercourse—all of this knowledge mastered surreptitiously, through observation alone, while moving about silently, camouflaged, *never asking for help.* You must become a part of the world you have entered, and the way to do it is to encourage a general assumption that you already are a part of it, have always been a part of it. Wherever you land, you need to recognize that life has been going on for millions of years, life goes on there steadily, with you or without you; you are the intrusive one, and if you don't want to feel intrusive you'd better learn fast how to fit in. Of course it isn't easy. The infiltrator doesn't have the privilege of buying stability by acting dumb. You won't be able to say, "How much does it cost to ride on the cable-car?" You won't be able to say, "I'm from somewhere else, and this is the kind of money I carry, dollars quarters pennies halves nickels, is any of it legal tender here?" You don't dare identify yourself in any way as an outsider. If you don't get the idioms or the accent right, you can tell them you grew up out of town, but that's as much as you can reveal. The truth is your eternal secret, even when you're in trouble, *especially* when you're in trouble. When your back's to the wall you won't have time to say, "Look, I wasn't born in this universe at all, you see, I came zipping in from some other place, so pardon me, forgive me, excuse me, pity me." No, no, no, you can't do that. They won't believe you, and even if they do, they'll make it all the worse for you once they know. If you want to infiltrate, Cameron, you've got to fake it all the way. Jaunty smile, steely even gaze. And you have to infiltrate. You know that, don't you? You don't really have any choice.

Infiltrating has its dangers too. The rough part comes when they find out, and they always do find you out. Then they'll react bitterly against your deception, they'll lash out in blind rage. If you're lucky, you'll be gone before they learn your sweaty little secret. Before they discover the discarded phrasebook hidden in the boarding-house room, before they stumble on the torn-off pages of your private journal. They'll find you out. They always do. But by then you'll be somewhere else, you hope, beyond the reach of their anger and their sorrow, beyond their reach, beyond their reach.

III

Suppose I show you, for Exhibit A, Cameron reacting to an extraordinary situation. You can test your own resilience by trying to picture yourself in his position. There has been a sensation in Cameron's mind very much like that of the extinction of the cosmos: a thunderclap, everything going black, a blankness, a total absence. Followed by the return of light, flowing inward upon him like high tide on the celestial shore, a surging stream of brightness moving with inexorable certainty. He stands flatfooted, dumbfounded, high on a bare hillside in warm early-hour sunlight. The house—redwood timbers, picture window, driftwood scriptures, paintings, books, records, refrigerator, gallon jugs of red wine, carpets, tiles, avocado plants in wooden tubs, carport, car, driveway—is gone. The neighboring houses are gone. The winding street is gone. The eucalyptus forest that ought to be behind him, rising toward the crest of the hill, is gone. Downslope there is no Oakland, there is no Berkeley, only a scattering of crude squatters' shacks running raggedly along unpaved switchbacks toward the pure blue bay. Across the water there is no Bay Bridge; on the far shore there is no San Francisco. The Golden Gate Bridge does not span the gap between the city and the Marin headland. Cameron is astonished, not that he didn't expect something like this, but that the transformation is so complete, so absolute. If you don't want your world any more, the old man had said, you can just drop it, can't you? Let go of it, let it drop. Can't you? Of course you can. And so Cameron has let go of it. He's in another place entirely, now. Wherever this place is, it isn't home. The sprawling Bay Area cities and towns aren't here, never were. Good-bye, San Leandro, San Mateo, El Cerrito, Walnut Creek. He sees a landscape of gentle bare hills, rolling meadows, the dry brown grass of summer; the scarring hand of man is evident only occasionally. He begins to adapt. This is what he must have wanted, after all, and though he has been jarred by the shock of transition he is recovering quickly, he is settling in, he feels already that he could belong here. He will explore this unfamiliar world and if he finds it good he will discover a niche for himself. The air is sweet. The sky is cloudless. Has he really gone to some new place, or is he still in the old place and has everything else that was there simply gone away? Easy. He has gone. Everything else has gone. The cosmos has entered into a transitional phase. Nothing's stable any more. From this moment onward, Cameron's existence is a conditional matter, subject to ready alteration. What did the old man say? Go wherever you like. Define your world as you would like it to be, and go there, and if you discover that you don't care for this or don't need that, why, go somewhere else. It's all trips, this universe. What else is there? There isn't anything but trips. Just trips. So here you are, friend. New frameworks! New patterns! New!

IV

There is a sound to his left, the crackling of dry brush underfoot, and Cameron turns, looking straight into the morning sun, and sees a man on horseback approaching him. He is tall, slender, about Cameron's own height and build, it seems, but perhaps a shade broader through the shoulders. His hair, like Cameron's, is golden, but it is much longer, descending in a straight flow to his shoulders and tumbling onto his chest. He has a soft, full, curling beard, untrimmed but tidy. He wears a wide-brimmed hat, buckskin chaps, and a light fringed jacket of tawny leather. Because of the sunlight Cameron has difficulty at first making out his features, but after a moment his eyes adjust and he sees that the other's face is very much like his own, thin lips, jutting high-bridged nose, clefted chin, cool blue eyes below heavy brows. Of course. Your face is my face. You and I, I and you, drawn to the same place at the same time across the many worlds. Cameron had not expected this, but now that it has happened it seems to have been inevitable.

They look at each other. Neither speaks. During that silent moment Cameron invents a scene for them. He imagines the other dismounting, inspecting him in wonder, walking around him, peering into his face, studying it, frowning, shaking his head, finally grinning and saying:

—I'll be damned. I never knew I had a twin brother. But here you are. It's just like looking in the mirror.
 —We aren't twins.
 —We've got the same face. Same everything. Trim away a little hair and nobody could tell me from you, you from me. If we aren't twins, what are we?
 —We're closer than brothers.
 —I don't follow your meaning, friend.
 —This is how it is. I'm you. You're me. One soul, one identity. What's your name?
 —Cameron.
 —Of course. First name?
 —Kit.
 —That's short for Christopher, isn't it? My name is Cameron too. Chris. Short for Christopher. I tell you, we're one and the same person, out of two different worlds. Closer than brothers. Closer than anything.

None of this is said, however. Instead the man in the leather clothing rides slowly toward Cameron, pauses, gives him a long, incurious stare, and says simply, "Morning. Nice day." And continues onward.
 "Wait," Cameron says.
 The man halts. Looks back. "What?"
 Never ask for help. Fake it all the way. Jaunty smile, steely even gaze.
 Yes. Cameron remembers all that. Somehow, though, infiltration seems easier to bring off in a city. You can blend into the background there. More difficult here, exposed as you are against the stark, unpeopled landscape.
 Cameron says, as casually as he can, using what he hopes is a colorless neutral accent, "I've been traveling out from inland. Came a long way."
 "Umm. Didn't you think you were from around here. Your clothes."

"Inland clothes."

"The way you talk. Different. So?"

"New to these parts. Wondered if you could tell me a place I could hire a room till I got settled."

"You come all this way on foot?"

"Had a mule. Lost him back in the valley. Lost everything I had with me."

"Umm. Indians cutting up again. You give them a little gin, they go crazy." The other smiles faintly; then the smile fades and he retreats into impassivity, sitting motionless with hands on thighs, face a mask of patience that seems merely to be a thin covering for impatience or worse.

—*Indians?*—

"They gave me a tough time," Cameron says, getting into the fantasy of it.

"Umm."

"Cleaned me out, let me go."

"Umm. Umm."

Cameron feels his sense of a shared identity with this man lessening. There is no way of engaging him. *I am you, you are I, and yet you take no notice of the strange fact that I wear your face and body, you seem to show no interest in me at all. Or else you hide your interest amazingly well.*

Cameron says, "You know where I can get lodging?"

"Nothing much around here. Not many settlers this side of the bay, I guess."

"I'm strong. I can do most any kind of work. Maybe you could use—"

"Umm. No." Cold dismissal glitters in the frosty eyes. Cameron wonders how often people in the world of his former life saw such a look in his own. A tug on the reins. *Your time is up, stranger.* The horse swings around and begins picking its way daintily along the path.

Desperately Cameron calls, "One thing more!"

"Umm?"

"Is your name Cameron?"

A flicker of interest. "Might be."

"Christopher Cameron. Kit. Chris. That you?"

"Kit." The other's eyes drill into his own. The mouth compresses until the lips are invisible: not a scowl but a speculative, pensive movement. There is tension in the way the other man grasps his reins. For the first time Cameron feels that he has made contact. "Kit Cameron, yes. Why?"

"Your wife," Cameron says. "Her name Elizabeth?"

The tension increases. The other Cameron is cloaked in explosive silence. Something terrible is building within him. Then, unexpectedly, the tension snaps. The other man spits, scowls, slumps in his saddle. "My woman's dead," he mutters. "Say, who the hell are you? What do you want with me?"

"I'm—I'm—" Cameron falters. He is overwhelmed by fear and pity. A bad start, a lamentable start. He trembles. He had not thought it would be anything like this. With an effort he masters himself. Fiercely he says, "I've got to know. Was her name Elizabeth?" For an answer the horseman whacks his heels savagely against his mount's ribs and gallops away, fleeing as though he had had an encounter with Satan.

V

Go, the old man said. You know the score. That is how it is: everything's random, nothing's fixed unless we want it to be, and even then the system isn't as stable as we think it is. So go. Go. Go, he said, and, of course, hearing something like that, Cameron went. What else could he do, once he had his freedom, but abandon his native universe and try a different one? Notice that I didn't say a better one, just a different one. Or two or three or five different ones. It was a gamble, certainly. He might lose everything that mattered to him, and gain nothing worth having. But what of it? Every day is full of gambles like that: you stake your life whenever you open a door. You never know what's heading your way, not ever, and still you choose to play the game. How can a man be expected to become all he's capable of becoming if he spends his whole life pacing up and down the same courtyard? Go. Make your voyages. Time forks, again and again and again. New universes split off at each instant of decision. Left turn, right turn, honk your horn, jump the traffic light, hit your gas, hit your brake, every action spawns whole galaxies of possibility. We move through a soup of infinities. If repressing a sneeze generates an alternative continuum, what, then, are the consequences of the truly major acts, the assassinations and inseminations, the conversions, the renunciations? Go. And as you travel, mull these thoughts constantly. Part of the game is discerning the precipitating factors that shaped the worlds you visit. What's the story here? Dirt roads, donkey-carts, hand-sewn clothes. No Industrial Revolution, is that it? The steam-engine man—what was his name, Savery, Newcomen, Watt?—smothered in his cradle? No mines, no factories, no assembly lines, no dark Satanic mills. That must be it. The air is so pure here: you can tell by that, it's a simpler era. Very good, Cameron. You see the patterns swiftly. But now try somewhere else. Your own self has rejected you here; besides, this place has no Elizabeth. Close your eyes. Summon the lightning.

VI

The parade has reached a disturbing level of frenzy. Marchers and floats now occupy the side streets as well as the main boulevard, and there is no way to escape from their demonic enthusiasm. Streamers cascade from office windows and gigantic photographs of Chairman DeGrasse have sprouted on every wall, suddenly, like dark infestations of lichen. A boy presses close against Cameron, extends a clenched fist, opens his fingers: on his palm rests a glittering jeweled case, egg-shaped, thumbnail-sized. "Spores from Patagonia," he says. "Let me have ten exchanges and they're yours." Politely Cameron declines. A woman in a blue and orange frock tugs at his arm and says urgently, "All the rumors are true, you know. They've just been confirmed. What are you going to do about that? What are you going to *do*?" Cameron shrugs and smiles and disengages himself. A man with gleaming buttons asks, "Are you enjoying the festival? I've sold everything and I'm going to move to the highway next Godsday." Cameron nods and murmurs congratulations, hoping congratulations are in order. He turns a corner and confronts, once more, the bishop who looks like Elizabeth's brother, who *is*, he concludes, indeed Elizabeth's brother. "Forget your sins!" he is crying still. "Cancel your debts!" Cameron thrusts his head between two plump girls at the curb and attempts to call to him, but his voice fails, nothing coming forth but a hoarse wordless rasp, and the bishop moves on. Moving on is a good idea, Cameron tells himself. This place exhausts him. He has come to it too soon, and its manic tonality is more than he wants to handle. He finds a quiet alleyway and presses his cheek against a cool brick wall, and stands there breathing deeply until he is calm enough to depart. All right. Onward.

VII

Empty grasslands spread to the horizon. This could be the Gobi steppe. Cameron sees neither cities nor towns nor even villagers, just six or seven squat black tents pitched in a loose circle in the saddle between two low gray-green hummocks, a few hundred yards from where he stands. He looks beyond, across the gently folded land, and spies dark animal figures at the limits of his range of vision: about a dozen horses, close together, muzzle to muzzle, flank to flank, horses with riders. Or perhaps they are a congregation of centaurs. Anything is possible. He decides, though, that they are Indians, a war party of young braves, maybe, camping in these desolate plains. They see him. Quite likely they saw him some while before he noticed them. Casually they break out of their grouping, wheel, ride in his direction.

He awaits them. Why should he flee? Where could he hide? Their pace accelerates from trot to canter, from canter to wild gallop; now they plunge toward him with fluid ferocity and a terrifying eagerness. They wear open leather jackets and rough rawhide leggings; they carry lances, bows, battle-axes, long curved swords; they ride small, agile horses, hardly more than ponies, tireless packets of energy. They surround him, pulling up, the fierce little steeds rearing and whinnying; they peer at him, point, laugh, exchange harsh derisive comments in a mysterious language. Then, solemnly, they begin to ride slowly in a wide circle around him. They are flat-faced, small-nosed, bearded, with broad, prominent cheekbones; the crowns of their heads are shaven, but long black hair streams down over their ears and the napes of their necks. Heavy folds in the upper lids give their eyes a slanted look. Their skins are copper-colored but with an underlying golden tinge, as though these were not Indians at all, but—what? Japanese? A samurai corps? No, probably not Japanese. But not Indians either.

They continue to circle him, gradually moving more swiftly. They chatter to one another and occasionally hurl what sounds like questions at him. They seem fascinated by him, but also contemptuous. In a sudden demonstration of horsemanship one of them cuts from the circular formation and, goading his horse to an instant gallop, streaks past Cameron, leaning down to jab a finger into his forearm. Then another does it, and another, streaking back and forth across the circle, poking him, plucking at his hair, tweaking him, nearly running him down. They draw their swords and swish them through the air just above his head. They menace him, or pretend to, with their lances. Throughout it all they laugh. He stands perfectly still. This ordeal, he suspects, is a test of his courage. Which he passes, eventually. The lunatic galloping ceases; they rein in, and several of them dismount.

They are little men, chest-high to him but thicker through the chest and shoulders than he is. One unships a leather pouch and offers it to him with an unmistakable gesture: take, drink. Cameron sips cautiously. It is a thick grayish fluid, both sweet and sour. Fermented milk? He gags, winces, forces himself to sip again; they watch him closely. The second taste isn't so bad. He takes a third more willingly and gravely returns the pouch.

The warriors laugh, not derisively now but more in applause, and the man who had given him the pouch slaps Cameron's shoulder admiringly. He tosses the pouch back to Cameron. Then he leaps to his saddle, and abruptly they all take off. Mongols, Cameron realizes. The sons of Genghis Khan, riding to the horizon. A worldwide empire? Yes, and this must be the wild west for them, the frontier, where the young men enact their rites of passage. Back in Europe, after seven centuries of Mongol dominance, they have become citified, domesticated, sippers of wine, theatergoers, cultivators of gardens, but here they follow the ways of their all-conquering forefathers. Cameron shrugs. Nothing for him here. He takes a last sip of the milk and drops the pouch into the tall grass. Onward.

VIII

No grass grows here. He sees the stumps of buildings, the blackened trunks of dead trees, mounds of broken tile and brick. The smell of death is in the air. All the bridges are down. Fog rolls in off the bay, dense and greasy, and becomes a screen on which images come alive. These ruins are inhabited. Figures move about. They are living dead. Looking into the thick mist he sees a vision of the shock wave, he recoils as alpha particles shower his skin. He beholds the survivors emerging from their shattered houses, straggling into the smoldering streets, naked, stunned, their bodies charred, their eyes glazed, some of them with their hair on fire. The walking dead. No one speaks. No one asks why this has happened. He is watching a silent movie. The apocalyptic fire has touched the ground here; the land itself is burning. Blue phosphorescent flames rise from the earth. The final judgment, the day of wrath. Now he hears a dread music beginning, a dead-march, all cellos and basses, the dark notes coming at wide intervals: ooom ooom ooom ooom ooom. And then the tempo picks up, the music becomes a danse macabre, syncopated, lively, the timbre still dark, the rhythms funereal: ooom ooom ooom-de-ooom de-ooom de-ooom de-ooom-de-ooom, jerky, chaotic, wildly gay. The distorted melody of the

"Ode to Joy" lurks somewhere in the ragged strands of sound. The dying victims stretch their fleshless hands toward him. He shakes his head. What service can I do for you? Guilt assails him. He is a tourist in the land of their grief. Their eyes reproach him. He would embrace them, but he fears they will crumble at his touch, and he lets the procession go past him without doing anything to cross the gulf between himself and them. "Elizabeth?" he murmurs. "Norman?" They have no faces, only eyes. "What can I do? I can't do anything for you." Not even tears will come. He looks away. Though I speak with the tongues of men and of angels, and have not charity, I am become as sounding brass, or a tinkling cymbal. And though I have the gift of prophecy, and understand all mysteries, and all knowledge; and though I have all faith, so that I could remove mountains, and have not charity, I am nothing. But this world is beyond the reach of love. He looks away. The sun appears. The fog burns off. The visions fade. He sees only the dead land, the ashes, the ruins. All right. Here we have no continuing city, but we seek one to come. Onward. Onward.

IX

And now, after this series of brief, disconcerting intermediate stops, Cameron has come to a city that is San Francisco beyond doubt, not some other city on San Francisco's site but a true San Francisco, a recognizable San Francisco. He pops into it atop Russian Hill, at the very crest, on a dazzling, brilliant, cloudless day. To his left, below, lies Fisherman's Wharf; ahead of him rises the Coit Tower, yes, and he can see the Ferry Building and the Bay Bridge. Familiar landmarks—but how strange all the rest seems! Where is the eye-stabbing Transamerica pyramid? Where is the colossal somber stalk of the Bank of America? The strangeness, he realizes, derives not so much from substitutions as from absences. The big Embarcadero developments are not there, nor the Chinatown Holiday Inn, nor the miserable tentacles of the elevated freeways, nor, apparently, anything else that was constructed in the last twenty years. This is the old short-shanked San Francisco of his boyhood, a sparkling miniature city, unManhattanized, skylineless. Surely he has returned to the place he knew in the sleepy 1950's, the tranquil Eisenhower years.

He heads downhill, searching for a newspaper box. He finds one at the corner of Hyde and North Point, a bright yellow metal rectangle. San Francisco *Chronicle,* ten cents. Ten cents? Is that the right price for 1954? One Roosevelt dime goes into the slot. The paper, he finds, is dated Tuesday, August 19, 1975. In what Cameron still thinks of, with some irony now, as the real world, the world that has been receding rapidly from him all day in a series of discontinuous jumps, it is also Tuesday, the 19th of August, 1975. So he has not gone backward in time at all; he has come to a San Francisco where time has seemingly been standing still. Why? In vertigo he eyes the front page.

A three-column headline declares:

FÜHRER ARRIVES IN WASHINGTON

Under it, to the left, a photograph of three men, smiling broadly, positively beaming at one another. The caption identifies them as President Kennedy, Führer Göring, and Ambassador Togarashi of Japan, meeting in the White House rose garden. Cameron closes his eyes. Using no data other than the headline and the caption, he attempts to concoct a plausible speculation. This is a world, he decides, in which the Axis must have won the war. The United States is a German fiefdom. There are no high-rise buildings in San Francisco because the American economy, shattered by defeat, has not yet in thirty years of peace returned to a level where it can afford to erect them, or perhaps because American venture capital, prodded by the financial ministers of the Third Reich—(Hjalmar Schacht? The name drifts out of the swampy recesses of memory)—now tends to flow toward Europe. But how could it have happened? Cameron remembers the war years clearly, the tremendous surge of patriotism, the vast mobilization, the great national effort. Rosie the Riveter. Lucky Strike Green Goes to War. Let's Remember Pearl Harbor, As We Did the Alamo. He doesn't see any way the Germans might have brought America to her knees. Except one. The bomb, he thinks, the bomb, the Nazis get the bomb in 1940 and Wernher von Braun invents a transatlantic rocket and New York and Washington are nuked one night and that's it, we've been pushed beyond the resources of patriotism, we cave in and surrender within a week. And so—

He studies the photograph. President Kennedy, grinning, standing between Reichsführer Göring and a suave youthful-looking Japanese. Kennedy? Ted? No, this is Jack, the very same Jack who, looking jowly, heavy bags under his eyes, deep creases in his face—he must be almost sixty years old, nearing the end of what is probably his second term of office. Jacqueline waiting none too patiently for him upstairs. Get done with your Japs and Nazis, love, and let's have a few drinkies together before the concert. Yes. John-John and Caroline somewhere on the premises too, the nation's darlings, models for young people everywhere. Yes. And Göring? Indeed, the very same Göring who. Well into his eighties, monstrously fat, chin upon chin, multitudes of chins, vast bemedaled bosom, little mischievous eyes glittering with a long lifetime's cheery recollections of gratified lusts. How happy he looks! And how amiable! It was always impossible to hate Göring the way one loathed Goebbels, say, or Himmler or Streicher; Göring had charm, the outrageous charm of a monstre sacré, of a Nero, of a Caligula, and here he is alive in the 1970's, a mountain of immortal flesh, having survived Adolf to become—Cameron assumes—Second Führer and to be received in pomp at the White House, no less. Perhaps a state banquet tomorrow night, rollmops, sauerbraten, Kasseler rippchen, Koenigsberger Klöpse, washed down with flagons of Bernkasteler Doktor '69, Schloss Johannisberg '71, or does the Führer prefer beer? We have the finest lagers on tap, Löwenbräu, Würzburger Hofbräu—

But wait. Something rings false in Cameron's historical construct. He is unable to find in John F. Kennedy those depths of opportunism that would allow him to serve as puppet President of a Nazi-ruled America, taking orders from some slick-haired hard-eyed gauleiter and hopping obediently when the Führer comes to town. Bomb or no bomb, there would have been a diehard underground resistance movement, decades of guerrilla warfare, bitter hatred of the German oppressor and of all collaborators. No surrender, then. The Axis has won the war, but the United States has retained its autonomy. Cameron revises his speculations. Suppose, he tells himself, Hitler in this universe did not break his pact with Stalin and invade Russia in the summer of 1941, but led his forces across the Channel instead to wipe out Britain. And the Japanese left Pearl Harbor alone, so the United States never was drawn into the war, which was over in fairly short order—say, by September of 1942. The Germans now rule Europe from Cornwall to the Urals, and the Japanese have the whole Pacific west of Hawaii; the United States, lost in dreamy neutrality, is an isolated nation, a giant Portugal, economically stagnant, largely cut off from the world trade. There are no skyscrapers in San Francisco because no one sees reason to build anything in this country. Yes? Is this how it is?

He seats himself on the stoop of a house and explores his newspaper. This world has a stock market, albeit a sluggish one: the Dow-Jones Industrials stand at 354.61. Some of the listings are familiar—IBM, AT&T, General Motors—but many are not. Litton, Syntex, and Polaroid all are missing; so is Xerox, but he finds its primordial predecessor, Haloid, in the quotations. There are two baseball leagues, each with eight clubs; the Boston Braves have moved to Milwaukee but otherwise the table of teams could have come straight out of the 1940s. Brooklyn is leading in the National League, Philadelphia in the American. In the news section he finds recognizable names: New York has a Senator Rockefeller, Massachusetts has a Senator Kennedy. (Robert, apparently. He is currently in Italy. Yesterday he toured the majestic Tomb of Mussolini near the Colosseum, today he has an audience with Pope Benedict.) An airline advertisement invites San Franciscans to go to New York via TWA's glorious new Starliners, now only twelve hours with just a brief stop in Chicago. The accompanying sketch indicates that they have about reached the DC-4 level here, or is that a DC-6, with all those propellers? The foreign news is tame and sketchy: not a word about Israel versus the Arabs, the squabbling republics of Africa, the People's Republic of China, or the war in South America. Cameron assumes that the only surviving Jews are those of New York and Los Angeles, that Africa is one immense German colonial tract with a few patches under Italian rule, that China is governed by the Japanese, not by the heirs of Chairman Mao, and that the South American nations are torpid and unaggressive. Yes? Reading this newspaper is the strangest experience this voyage has given him so far, for the pages *look* right, the tone of the writing *feels* right, there is the insistent texture of unarguable reality about the whole paper, and yet everything is subtly off, everything has undergone a slight shift along the spectrum of events. The newspaper has the quality of a dream, but he has never known a dream to have such overwhelming substantive density.

He folds the paper under his arm and strolls toward the bay. A block from the waterfront he finds a branch of the Bank of America—some things withstand all permutations—and goes inside to change some money. There are risks, but he is curious. The teller unhesitatingly takes his five-dollar bill and hands him four singles and a little stack of coins. The singles are unremarkable, and Lincoln, Jefferson, and Washington occupy their familiar places on the cent, nickel, and quarter; but the dime shows Ben Franklin and the fifty-cent piece bears the features of a hearty-looking man, youngish, full-faced, bushy-haired, whom Cameron is unable to identify at all.

On the next corner eastward he comes to a public library. Now he can confirm his guesses. An almanac! Yes, and how odd the list of Presidents looks. Roosevelt, he learns, retired in poor health in 1940, and that, so far as he can discover, is the point of divergence between this world and his. The rest follows predictably enough. Wendell Willkie, defeating John Nance Garner in the 1940 election, maintains a policy of strict neutrality while—yes, it was as he had imagined—the Germans and Japanese quickly conquer most of the world. Willkie dies in office during the 1944 Presidential campaign—aha! That's Willkie on the half-dollar!—and is briefly succeeded by Vice President McNary, who does not want the Presidency; a hastily recalled Republican convention nominates Robert Taft. Two terms then for Taft, who beats James Byrnes, and two for Thomas Dewey, and then in 1960 the long Republican era is ended at last by Senator Lyndon Johnson of Texas. Johnson's running mate—it is an amusing reversal, Cameron thinks—is Senator John F. Kennedy of Massachusetts. After the traditional two terms, Johnson steps down and Vice President Kennedy wins the 1968 Presidential election. He has been re-elected in 1972, naturally; in this placid world incumbents always win. There is, of course, no UN here; there has been no Korean war, no movement of colonial liberation, no exploration of space. The almanac tells Cameron that Hitler lived until 1960, Mussolini until 1958. The world seems to have adapted remarkably readily to Axis rule, although a German army of occupation is still stationed in England.

He is tempted to go on and on, comparing histories, learning the transmuted destinies of such figures as Hubert Humphrey, Dwight Eisenhower, Harry Truman, Nikita Khruschchev, Lee Harvey Oswald, Juan Peron. But suddenly a more intimate curiosity flowers in him. In a hallway alcove he consults the telephone book. There is one directory covering both Alameda and Contra Costa counties, and it is a much more slender volume than the directory which in his world covers Oakland alone. There are two dozen Cameron listings, but none at his address, and no Christophers or Elizabeths or any plausible permutations of those names. On a hunch he looks in the San Francisco book. Nothing promising there either; but then he checks Elizabeth under her maiden name, Dudley, and yes, there is an Elizabeth Dudley at the familiar old address on Laguna. The discovery causes him to tremble. He rummages in his pocket, finds his Ben Franklin dime, drops it in the slot. He listens. There's the dial tone. He makes the call.

X

The apartment, what he can see of it by peering past her shoulder, looks much as he remembers it: well-worn couches and chairs upholstered in burgundy and dark green, stark whitewashed walls, elaborate sculptures—her own—of gray driftwood, huge ferns in hanging containers. To behold these objects in these surroundings wrenches powerfully at his sense of time and place and afflicts him with an almost unbearable nostalgia. The last time he was here, if indeed he has ever been "here" in any sense, was in 1969; but the memories are vivid, and what he sees corresponds so closely to what he recalls that he feels transported to that earlier era. She stands in the doorway, studying him with cool curiosity tinged with unmistakable suspicion. She wears unexpectedly ordinary clothes, a loose-fitting embroidered white blouse and a short, pleated blue skirt, and her golden hair looks dull and carelessly combed, but surely she is the same woman from whom he parted this morning, the same woman with whom he has shared his life these past seven years, a beautiful woman, a tall woman, nearly as tall as he—on some occasions taller, it has seemed—with a serene smile and steady green eyes and smooth, taut skin. "Yes?" she says uncertainly. "Are you the man who phoned?"

"Yes. Chris Cameron." He searches her face for some flicker of recognition. "You don't know me? Not at all?"

"Not at all. Should I know you?"

"Perhaps. Probably not. It's hard to say."

"Have we once met? Is that it?"

"I'm not sure how I'm going to explain my relationship to you."

"So you said when you called. Your *relationship* to me? How can strangers have had a relationship?"

"It's complicated. May I come in?"

She laughs nervously, as though caught in some embarrassing faux pas. "Of course," she says, not without giving him a quick appraisal, making a rapid estimate of risk. The apartment is in fact almost exactly as he knew it, except that there is no stereo phonograph, only a bulky archaic Victrola, and her record collection is surprisingly scanty, and there are rather fewer books than his Elizabeth would have had. They confront one another stiffly. He is as uneasy over this encounter as she is, and finally it is she who seeks some kind of social lubricant, suggesting that they have a little wine. She offers him red or white.

"Red, please," he says.

She goes to a low sideboard and takes out two cheap, clumsy-looking tumblers. Then, effortlessly, she lifts a gallon jug of wine from the floor and begins to unscrew its cap. "You were awfully mysterious on the phone," she says, "and you're still being mysterious now. What brings you here? Do we have mutual friends?"

"I think it wouldn't be untruthful to say that we do. At least in a manner of speaking."

"Your own manner of speaking is remarkably roundabout, Mr. Cameron."

"I can't help that right now. And call me Chris, please." As she pours the wine he watches her closely, thinking of that other Elizabeth, *his* Elizabeth, thinking how well he knows her body, the supple play of muscles in her back, the sleek texture of her skin, the firmness of her flesh, and he flashes instantly to their strange, absurdly romantic meeting years ago, that June when he had gone off alone into the Sierra high country for a week of backpacking and, following heaps of stones that he had wrongly taken to be trail-markers, had come to a place well off the path, a private place, a cool dark glacial lake rimmed by brilliant patches of late-lying snow, and had begun to make camp, and had become suddenly aware of someone else's pack thirty yards away, and a pile of discarded clothing on the shore, and then had seen her, swimming just beyond a pine-tipped point, heading toward land, rising like Venus from the water, naked, noticing him, startled by his presence, apprehensive for a moment but then immediately making the best of it, relaxing, smiling, standing unashamed shin-deep in the chilly shallows and inviting him to join her for a swim. These recollections of that first contact and all that ensued excite him terribly, for this person before him is at once the Elizabeth he loves, familiar, joined to him by the bond of shared experience, and also someone new, a complete stranger, from whom he can draw fresh inputs, that jolting gift of novelty which his Elizabeth can never again offer him. He stares at her shoulders and back with fierce, intense hunger; she turns toward him with the glasses of wine in her hands, and, before he can mask that wild gleam of desire, she receives it with full force. The impact is immediate. She recoils. She is not the Elizabeth of the Sierra lake; she seems unable to handle such a level of unexpected erotic voltage. Jerkily she thrusts the wine at him, her hands shaking so that she spills a little on her sleeve. He takes the glass and backs away, a bit dazed by his own frenzied upwelling of emotion. With an effort he calms himself. There is a long moment of awkward silence while they drink. The psychic atmosphere grows less torrid; a certain mood of remote, businesslike courtesy develops between them.

After the second glass of wine she says, "Now. How do you know me and what do you want from me?"

Briefly he closes his eyes. What can he tell her? How can he explain? He has rehearsed no strategies. Already he has managed to alarm her with a single unguarded glance; what effect would a confession of apparent madness have? But he has never used strategies with Elizabeth, has never resorted to any tactics except the tactic of utter candidness. And this is

Elizabeth. Slowly he says, "In another existence you and I are married, Elizabeth. We live in the Oakland hills and we're extraordinarily happy together."

"Another existence?"

"In a world apart from this, a world where history took a different course a generation ago, where the Axis lost the war, where John Kennedy was President in 1963 and was killed by an assassin, where you and I met beside a lake in the Sierra and fell in love. There's an infinity of worlds, Elizabeth, side by side, worlds in which all possible variations of every possible event take place. Worlds in which you and I are married happily, in which you and I have been married and divorced, in which you and I don't exist, in which you exist and I don't, in which we meet and loathe one another, in which—in which—do you see, Elizabeth, there's a world for everything, and I've been traveling from world to world. I've seen nothing but wilderness where San Francisco ought to be, and I've met Mongol horsemen in the East Bay hills, and I've seen this whole area devastated by atomic warfare, and—does this sound insane to you, Elizabeth?"

"Just a little." She smiles. The old Elizabeth, cool, judicious, performing one of her specialties, the conditional acceptance of the unbelievable for the sake of some amusing conversation. "But go on. You've been jumping from world to world. I won't even bother to ask you how. What are you running away from?"

"I've never seen it that way. I'm running *toward*."

"Toward what?"

"An infinity of worlds. An endless range of possible experience."

"That's a lot to swallow. Isn't one world enough for you to explore?"

"Evidently not."

"You had all infinity," she says. "Yet you chose to come to me. Presumably I'm the one point of familiarity for you in this otherwise strange world. Why come here? What's the point of your wanderings, if you seek the familiar? If all you wanted to do was find your way back to your Elizabeth, why did you leave her in the first place? Are you as happy with her as you claim to be?"

"I can be happy with her and still desire her in other guises."

"You sound driven."

"No," he says. "No more driven than Faust. I believe in searching as a way of life. Not searching *for*, just searching. And it's impossible to stop. To stop is to die, Elizabeth. Look at Faust, going on and on, going to Helen of Troy herself, experiencing everything the world has to offer, and always seeking more. When Faust finally cries out, *This is it, this is what I've been looking for, this is where I choose to stop,* Mephistopheles wins his bet."

"But that was Faust's moment of supreme happiness."

"True. When he attains it, though, he loses his soul to the devil, remember?"

"So you go on, on and on, world after world, seeking you know not what, just seeking, unable to stop. And yet you claim you're not driven."

He shakes his head. "Machines are driven. Animals are driven. I'm an autonomous human being operating out of free will. I don't make this journey because I have to, but because I want to."

"Or because you think you ought to want to."

"I'm motivated by feelings, not by intellectual calculations and preconceptions."

"That sounds very carefully thought out," she tells him. He is stung by her words, and looks away, down into his empty glass. She indicates that he should help himself to the wine. "I'm sorry," she says, her tone softening a little.

He says, "At any rate, I was in the library and there was a telephone directory and I found you. This is where you used to live in my world, too, before we were married." He hesitates. "Do you mind if I ask—"

"What?"

"You're not married?"

"No. I live alone. And like it."

"You always were independent-minded."

"You talk as though you know me so well."

"I've been married to you for seven years."

"No. Not to me. Never to me. You don't know me at all."

He nods. "You're right. I don't really know you, Elizabeth, however much I think I do. But I want to. I feel drawn to you as strongly as I was to the other Elizabeth, that day in the mountains. It's always best right at the beginning, when two strangers reach toward one another, when the spark leaps the gap—" Tenderly he says, "May I spend the night here?"

"No."

Somehow the refusal comes as no surprise. He says, "You once gave me a different answer when I asked you that."

"Not I. Someone else."

"I'm sorry. It's so hard for me to keep you and her distinct in my mind, Elizabeth. But please don't turn me away. I've come so far to be with you."

"You came uninvited. Besides, I'd feel so strange with you—knowing you were thinking of her, comparing me with her, measuring our differences, our points of similarities—"

"What makes you think I would?"

"You would."

"I don't think that's sufficient reason for sending me away."

"I'll give you another," she says. Her eyes sparkle mischievously. "I never let myself get involved with married men."

She is teasing him now. He says, laughing, confident that she is beginning to yield, "That's the damnedest far-fetched excuse I've ever heard, Elizabeth!"

"Is it? I feel a great kinship with her. She has all my sympathies. Why should I help you deceive her?"

"Deceive? What an old-fashioned word! Do you think she'd object? She never expected me to be chaste on this trip. She'd be flattered and delighted to know that I went looking for you here. She'd be eager to hear about everything that went on between us. How could she possibly be hurt by knowing that I had been with you, when you and she are—"

"Nevertheless, I'd like you to leave. Please."

"You haven't given me one convincing reason."

"I don't need to."

"I love you. I want to spend the night with you."

"You love someone else who resembles me," she replies. "I keep telling you that. In any case, I don't love you. I don't find you attractive, I'm afraid."

"Oh. She does, but you—don't. I see. How do you find me, then? Ugly? Overbearing? Repellent?"

"I find you disturbing," she says. "A little frightening. Much too intense, much too controlled, perhaps dangerous. You aren't my type. I'm probably not yours. Remember, I'm not the Elizabeth you met by that mountain lake. Perhaps I'd be happier if I were, but I'm not. I wish you had never come here. Now: please go. Please."

XI

Onward. This place is all gleaming towers and airy bridges, a glistening fantasy of a city. High overhead float glassy bubbles, silent airborne passenger vehicles, containing two or three people apiece who sprawl in postures of elegant relaxation. Bronzed young boys and girls lie naked beside soaring fountains spewing turquoise-and-scarlet foam. Giant orchids burst in tropical voluptuousness from the walls of colossal hotels. Small mechanical birds wheel and dart in the soft air like golden bullets, emitting sweet pinging sounds. From the tips of the tallest buildings comes a darker music, a ground-bass of swelling hundred-cycle notes oscillating around an insistent central rumble. This is a world two centuries ahead of his, at the least. He could never infiltrate here. He could never even be a tourist. The only role available to him is that of visiting savage, Jemmy Button among the Londoners, and what, after all, was Jemmy Button's fate? Not a happy one. Patagonia! Patagonia! Thees ticket eet ees no longer good here, sor. Colored rays dance in the sky, red, green, blue, exploding, showering the city with transcendental images. Cameron smiles. He will not let himself be overwhelmed, though this place is more confusing than the world of the halftrack automobiles. Jauntily he plants himself at the center of a small park between two lanes of flowing noiseless traffic. It is a formal garden lush with toothy orange-fronded ferns and thorny skyrockets of looping cactus. Lovers stroll past him arm in arm, offering one another swigs from glossy sweat-beaded green flasks that look like tubes of polished jade. Delicately they dangle blue grapes before each other's lips, playfully they smile, arch their necks, take the bait with eager pounces; then they laugh, embrace, tumble into the dense moist grass, which stirs and sways and emits gentle thrumming melodies. This place pleases him. He wanders through the garden, thinking of Elizabeth, thinking of springtime, and, coming ultimately to a sinuous brook in which the city's tallest towers are reflected as inverted needles, he kneels to drink. The water is cool, sweet, tart, much like young wine. A moment after it touches his lips a mechanism rises from the spongy earth, five slender brassy columns, three with eye-sensors sprouting on all sides, one marked with a pattern of dark gridwork, one bearing an arrangement of winking colored lights. Out of the gridwork come ominous words in an unfathomable language. This is some kind of police machine, demanding his credentials: that much is clear. "I'm sorry," he says. "I can't understand what you're saying." Other machines are extruding themselves from trees, from the bed of the stream, from the hearts of the sturdiest ferns. "It's all right," he says. "I don't mean any harm. Just give me a chance to learn the language and I promise to become a useful citizen." One of the machines sprays him with a fine azure mist. Another drives a tiny needle into his forearm and extracts a droplet of blood. A crowd is gathering. They point, snicker, wink. The music of the building-tops has become higher in pitch, more sinister in texture; it shakes the balmy air and threatens him in a personal way. "Let me stay," Cameron begs, but the music is shoving him, pushing him with a flat irresistible hand, inexorably squeezing him out of this world. He is too primitive for them. He is too coarse, he carries too many obsolete microbes. Very well. If that's what they want, he'll leave, not out of fear, not because they've succeeded in intimidating him, but out of courtesy alone. In a flamboyant way he bids them farewell, bowing with a flourish worthy of Raleigh, blowing a kiss to the five-columned machine, smiling, even doing a little dance. Farewell. Farewell. The music rises to a wild crescendo. He hears celestial trumpets and distant thunder. Farewell. Onward.

XII

Here some kind of oriental marketplace has sprung up, foul-smelling, cluttered, medieval. Swarthy old men, white-bearded, in thick gray robes, sit patiently behind open burlap sacks of spices and grains. Lepers and cripples roam everywhere, begging importunately. Slender long-legged men wearing only tight loincloths and jingling dangling earrings of bright copper stalk through the crowd on solitary orbits, buying nothing, saying nothing; their skins are dark red, their faces are gaunt, their solemn features are finely modeled. They carry themselves like Inca princes. Perhaps they *are* Inca princes. In the haggle and babble of the market Cameron hears no recognizable tongue spoken. He sees the flash of gold as transactions are completed. The women balance immense burdens on their heads and show brilliant teeth when they smile. They favor patchwork skirts that cover their ankles, but they leave their breasts bare. Several of them glance provocatively at Cameron but he dares not return their quick dazzling probes until he knows what is permissible here. On the far side of the squalid plaza he catches sight of a woman who might well be Elizabeth; her back is to him, but he would know those strong shoulders anywhere, that erect stance, that cascade of unbound golden hair. He starts toward her, sliding with difficulty between the close-packed marketgoers. When he is still halfway across the marketplace from her he notices a man at her side, tall, a man of his own height and build. He wears a loose black robe and a dark scarf covers the lower half of his face. His eyes are grim and sullen and a terrible cicatrix, wide and glaringly crosshatched with stitchmarks, runs along his left cheek up to his hairline. The man whispers something to the woman who might be Elizabeth; she nods and turns, so that Cameron now is able to see her face, and yes, the woman does seem to be Elizabeth, but she bears a matching scar, angry and hideous, up the right side of her face. Cameron gasps. The scar-faced man suddenly points and shouts. Cameron senses motion to one side, and swings around just in time to see a short, thick-bodied man come rushing toward him wildly waving a scimitar. For an instant Cameron sees the scene as though in a photograph: he has time to make a leisurely examination of his attacker's oily beard, his hooked hairy-nostriled nose, his yellowed teeth, the cheap glassy-looking inlaid stones on the haft of the scimitar. Then the frightful blade descends, while the assassin screams abuse at Cameron in what might be Arabic. It is a sorry welcome. Cameron cannot prolong this investigation. An instant before the scimitar cuts him in two he takes himself elsewhere, with regret.

XIII

Onward. To a place where there is no solidarity, where the planet itself has vanished, so that he swims through space, falling peacefully, going from nowhere to nowhere. He is surrounded by a brilliant green light that emanates from every point at once, like a message from the fabric of the universe. In great tranquility he drops through this cheerful glow for days on end, or what seems like days on end, drifting, banking, checking his course with small motions of his elbows or knees. It makes no difference where he goes; everything here is like everything else here. The green glow supports and sustains and nourishes him, but it makes him restless. He plays with it. Out of its lambent substance he succeeds in shaping images, faces, abstract patterns; he conjures up Elizabeth for himself, he evokes his own sharp features, he fills the heavens with a legion of marching Chinese in tapered straw hats, he obliterates them with forceful diagonal lines, he causes a river of silver to stream across the firmament and discharge its glittering burden down a mountainside a thousand miles high. He spins. He floats. He glides. He releases all his fantasies. This is total freedom here in this unworldly place. But it is not enough. He grows weary of emptiness. He grows weary of serenity. He has drained this place of all it has to offer, too soon, too soon. He is not sure whether the failure is in himself or in the place, but he feels he must leave. Therefore: onward.

XIV

Terrified peasants run shrieking as he materializes in their midst. This is some sort of farming village along the eastern shore of the bay: neat green fields, a cluster of low wicker huts radiating from a central plaza, naked children toddling and crying, a busy sub-population of goats and geese and chickens. It is midday; Cameron sees the bright gleam of water in the irrigation ditches. These people work hard. They have scattered at his approach, but now they creep back warily, crouching, ready to take off again if he performs any more miracles. This is another of those bucolic worlds in which San Francisco has not happened, but he is unable to identify these settlers, nor can he isolate the chain of events that brought them here. They are not Indians, nor Chinese, nor Peruvians; they have a European look about them, somehow Slavic, but what would Slavs be doing in California? Russian farmers, maybe, colonizing by way of Siberia? There is some plausibility in that—their dark complexions, their heavy facial structure, their squat powerful bodies—but they seem oddly primitive, half-naked, in furry leggings or less, as though they were no subjects of the Tsar but rather Scythians or Cimmerians transplanted from the plains north of the Black Sea.

"Don't be frightened," he tells them, holding his upraised outspread arms toward them. They do seem less fearful of him now, timidly approaching, staring with big dark eyes. "I won't harm you. I'd just like to visit with you." They murmur. A woman boldly shoves a child forward, a girl of about five, bare, with black greasy ringlets, and Cameron scoops her up, caresses her, tickles her, lightly sets her down. Instantly the whole tribe is around him, no longer afraid; they touch his arm, they kneel, they stroke his shins. A boy brings him a wooden bowl of porridge. An old woman gives him a mug of sweet wine, a kind of mead. A slender girl drapes a stole of auburn fur over his shoulders. They dance, they chant; their fear has turned into love; he is their honored guest. He is more than that: he is a god. They take him to an unoccupied hut, the largest in the village. Piously they bring him offerings of incense and acorns. When it grows dark they build an immense bonfire in the plaza, so that he wonders in vague concern if they will feast on him when they are done honoring him, but they feast on slaughtered cattle instead, and yield to him the choicest pieces, and afterward they stand by his door, singing discordant, energetic hymns. That night three girls of the tribe, no doubt the fairest virgins available, are sent to him, and in the morning he finds his threshold heaped with newly plucked blossoms. Later two tribal artisans, one lame and the other blind, set to work with stone adzes and chisels, hewing an immense and remarkably accurate likeness of him out of a redwood stump that has been mounted at the plaza's center.

So he has been deified. He has a quick Faustian vision of himself living among these diligent people, teaching them advanced methods of agriculture, leading them eventually into technology, into modern hygiene, into all the contemporary advantages without the contemporary abominations. Guiding them toward the light, molding them, creating them. This world, this village would be a good place for him to stop his transit of the infinities, if stopping were desirable: god, prophet, king of a placid realm, teacher, inculcator of civilization, a purpose to his existence at last. But there *is* no place to stop. He knows that. Transforming happy primitive farmers into sophisticated twentieth-century agriculturalists is ultimately as useless a pastime as training fleas to jump through hoops. It is tempting to live as a god, but even divinity will pall, and it is dangerous to become attached to an unreal satisfaction, dangerous to become attached at all. The journey, not the arrival, matters. Always.

So Cameron does godhood for a little while. He finds it pleasant and fulfilling. He savors the rewards until he senses that the rewards are becoming too important to him. He makes his formal renunciation of his godhead. Then: onward.

XV

And this place he recognizes. His street, his house, his garden, his green car in the carport, Elizabeth's yellow one parked out front. Home again, so soon? He hadn't expected that; but every leap he has made, he knows, must in some way have been a product of deliberate choice, and evidently whatever hidden mechanism within him that has directed these voyages has chosen to bring him home again. All right, touch base. Digest your travels, examine them, allow your experiences to work their alchemy on you: you need to stand still a moment for that. Afterward you can always leave again. He slides his key into the door.

Elizabeth has one of the Mozart quartets on the phonograph. She sits curled up in the living-room window seat, leafing through a magazine. It is late afternoon and the San Francisco skyline, clearly visible across the bay through the big window, is haloed by the brilliant retreating sunlight. There are freshly cut flowers in the little crystal bowl on the redwood-burl table; the fragrance of gardenias and jasmines dances past him. Unhurriedly she looks up, brings her eyes into line with his, dazzles him with the warmth of her smile, and says, "Well, hello!"

"Hello, Elizabeth."

She comes to him. "I didn't expect you back this quickly, Chris. I don't know if I expected you to come back at all, as a matter of fact."

"This quickly? How long have I been gone, for you?"

"Tuesday morning to Thursday afternoon. Two and a half days." She eyes his coarse new beard, his ragged, sun-bleached shirt. "It's been longer for you, hasn't it?"

"Weeks and weeks. I'm not sure how long. I was in eight or nine different places, and I stayed in the last one quite some time. They were villagers, farmers, some primitive Slavonic tribe living down by the bay. I was their god, but I got bored with it."

"You always did get bored so easily," she says, and laughs, and takes his hands in hers and pulls him toward her. She brushes her lips lightly against him, a peck, a play-kiss, their usual first greeting, and then they kiss more passionately, bodies pressing close, tongue seeking tongue. He feels a pounding in his chest, the old inextinguishable throb. When they release each other he steps back, a little dizzied, and says, "I missed you, Elizabeth. I didn't know how much I'd miss you until I was somewhere else and aware that I might never find you again."

"Did you seriously worry about that?"

"Very much."

"I never doubted we'd be together again, one way or another. Infinity's such a big place, darling. You'd find your way back to me, or to someone very much like me. And someone very much like you would find his way to me, if you didn't. How many Chris Camerons do you think there are, on the move between worlds right now? A thousand? A trillion trillion?" She turns toward the sideboard and says, without breaking the flow of her words, "Would you like some wine?" and begins to pour from a half-empty jug of red. "Tell me where you've been," she says.

He comes up behind her and rests his hands on her shoulders, and draws them down the back of her silk blouse to her waist, holding her there, kissing the nape of her neck. He says, "To a world where there was an atomic war here, and to one where there still were Indian raiders out by Livermore, and one that was all fantastic robots and futuristic helicopters, and one where

Johnson was President before Kennedy and Kennedy is alive and President now, and one where—oh, I'll give you all the details later. I need a chance to unwind first." He releases her and kisses the tip of her earlobe and takes one of the glasses from her, and they salute each other and drink, draining the wine quickly. "It's so good to be home," he says softly. "Good to have gone where I went, good to be back." She fills his glass again. The familiar domestic ritual: red wine is their special drink, cheap red wine out of gallon jugs. A sacrament, more dear to him than the burnt offerings of his recent subjects. Halfway through the second glass he says, "Come. Let's go inside."

The bed has fresh linens on it, cool, inviting. There are three thick books on the night table: she's set up for some heavy reading in his absence. Cut flowers in here, too, fragrance everywhere. Their clothes drop away. She touches his beard and chuckles at the roughness, and he kisses the smooth cool place along the inside of her thigh and draws his cheek lightly across it, sandpapering her lovingly, and then she pulls him to her and their bodies slide together and he enters her. Everything thereafter happens quickly, much too quickly; he has been long absent from her, if not she from him, and now her presence excites him, there is a strangeness about her body, her movements, and it hastens him to his ecstasy. He feels a mild pang of regret, but no more: he'll make it up to her soon enough, they both know that. They drift into a sleepy embrace, neither of them speaking, and eventually uncoil into tender new passion, and this time all is as it should be. Afterward they doze. A spectacular sunset glazes over the city when he opens his eyes. They rise, they take a shower together, much giggling, much playfulness. "Let's go across the bay for a fancy dinner tonight," he suggests. "Trianon, Blue Fox, Ernie's, anywhere. You name it. I feel like celebrating."

"So do I, Chris."

"It's good to be home again."

"It's good to have you here," she tells him. She looks for her purse. "How soon do you think you'll be heading out again? Not that I mean to rush you, but—"

"You know I'm not going to be staying?"

"Of course I know."

"Yes. You would." She had never questioned his going. They both tried to be responsive to each other's needs; they had always regarded one another as equal partners, free to do as they wished. "I can't say how long I'll stay. Probably not long. Coming home this soon was really an accident, you know. I just planned to go on and on and on, world after world, and I never programmed my next jump, at least not consciously. I simply leaped. And the last leap deposited me on my own doorstep, somehow, so I let myself into the house. And there you were to welcome me home."

She presses his hand between hers. Almost sadly she says, "You aren't home, Chris."

"What?"

He hears the sound of the front door opening. Footsteps in the hallway.

"You aren't home," she says.

Confusion seizes him. He thinks of all that has passed between them this evening.

"Elizabeth?" calls a deep voice from the living room.

"In here, darling. I have company."

"Oh? Who?" A man enters the bedroom, halts, grins. He is clean-shaven and dressed in the clothes Cameron had worn on Tuesday; otherwise they could be twins. "Hey, hello!" he says warmly, extending his hand.

Elizabeth says, "He comes from a place that must be very much like this one. He's been here since five o'clock, and we were just going out for dinner. Have you been having an interesting time?"

"Very," the other Cameron says. "I'll tell you all about it later. Go on, don't let me keep you."

"You could join us for dinner," Cameron suggests helplessly.

"That's all right. I've just eaten. Breast of passenger pigeon—they aren't extinct everywhere. I wish I could have brought some home for the freezer. So you two go and enjoy. I'll see you later. Both of you, I hope. Will you be staying with us? We've got notes to compare, you and I."

XVI

He rises just before dawn, in a marvelous foggy stillness. The Camerons have been wonderfully hospitable, but he must be moving along. He scrawls a thank-you note and slips it under their bedroom door. *Let's get together again someday. Somewhere. Somehow.* They want him as a house guest for a week or two, but no, he feels like a bit of an intruder here, and anyway the universe is waiting for him. He has to go. The journey, not the arrival, matters, for what else is there but trips? Departing is unexpectedly painful, but he knows the mood will pass. He closes his eyes. He breaks his moorings. He gives himself up to his sublime restlessness. Onward. Onward. *Good-bye, Elizabeth. Good-bye, Chris. I'll see you both again. Onward.*